Anger tightened his mouth.

'You deliberately set out to seduce me in order to get pregnant, didn't you?'

She met his eyes, blazing with fury and hurt, and hated herself.

'Yes,' she told him quietly. 'I did.'

'Well, get this, Melissa. There's no way your little plan is going to work, because I intend to be involved every single step of the way, from now onwards for the next thirty or forty years. You can forget any ideas you had about bringing it up alone, do you understand? Because that's my baby!'

Caroline Anderson's nursing career was brought to an abrupt halt by a back injury, but her interest in medical things led her to work first as a medical secretary, and then, after completing her teacher training, as a lecturer in Medical Office Practice to trainee medical secretaries. She lives in rural Suffolk, with her husband, two daughters, mother and assorted animals.

Recent titles by the same author:

THAT'S MY BABY!

BY
CAROLINE ANDERSON

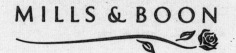

MILLS & BOON

*MILLS & BOON, the Rose Device and
LOVE ON CALL are trademarks of the publisher.
Harlequin Mills & Boon Limited,
Eton House, 18-24 Paradise Road, Richmond, Surrey TW9 1SR
This edition published by arrangement with Harlequin Enterprises B.V.*

© Caroline Anderson 1995

ISBN 0 263 79403 2

*Set in Times 10 on 11 pt. by
Rowland Phototypesetting Limited
Bury St Edmunds, Suffolk*

03-9512-47760

*Made and printed in Great Britain
Cover illustration by Simon Bishop*

PROLOGUE

'YOU'VE done *what*?'

Josh studied his brother—the eyes that wouldn't quite meet his own, the lower lip being absently gnawed while his mind scrambled for words to explain his way out—while Josh himself grappled with the 'birthday present' he had just been handed.

'Michael?' Josh prompted, his tone a mixture of frustration and resignation.

His brother shrugged helplessly. 'We couldn't think of anything you needed more,' he said finally, as if that made it any better.

'Needed. . .! Michael, I don't believe you really did this to me! I *need* this present like I need a hole in the head!'

Mike Lancaster took a deep breath, raised his head and finally met his brother's glowering eyes. 'Just give it a try, Josh. It won't cost you anything——'

'Cost? Damn it, Mike, money has nothing to do with it! I've been manoeuvred—manipulated!'

'Oh, for God's sake, bro, chill out! All I've done is register you with a dating agency. If you don't want to, you don't even have to contact any of the women they offer you. Stop over-reacting.'

'Too damn right I'm over-reacting! I think I have a right to! What if they contact me? Have you thought about that?'

Mike shrugged. 'They can't contact you direct—and anyway, you might get lucky.'

Josh gave a disbelieving snort. 'And pigs fly.'

'I met Ellie.'

The silence stretched out, their eyes locked, and then finally Josh shrugged. 'So you were lucky. The one in a million—and anyway, it doesn't count, she works there. What the hell makes you think I'd find anyone? I've got more chance of winning the National Lottery.' He rammed long, straight fingers through his unruly not-quite-black hair and let his breath out in a harsh sigh. 'I'm OK, Mike. Really. I don't need anyone.'

'Of course you do. You're lonely, bored, your personal life's a wasteland. Nobody's an island, Josh. We all need someone.'

Josh felt his brother's words twist something deep inside his chest—something he had been trying to ignore for years now. He fell back on the old excuse. 'I haven't got time.'

'Of course you have.'

'No.'

'Yes. Everyone has time—anyway, you'll have more soon, when you get a senior registrar's post.'

Josh snorted. 'If I do.'

'With your qualifications? Don't be silly, of course you will, and then you'll have all that time on your hands and no one to spend it with.'

There was a silence. Josh felt the pain inside, the old, familiar ache of loneliness. Was it so obvious? It wasn't as if he'd ever loved and lost, not really. There had never been anyone important in his life apart from his family. Mike was probably his closest friend, as well as his brother. In fact, since Mike had found happiness with Ellie, Josh's own loneliness had increased, whether because of the loss of his brother's companionship or because Josh had watched their relationship blossom and grow and seen first-hand what was missing in his own life he couldn't be sure. Probably both——

'Give it a try, Josh? Please?'

He met his brother's eyes and saw the genuine love and concern in them, and felt a lump form in his throat. 'OK, dammit—I'll try, if it'll shut you up. But don't expect miracles.'

Mike's anxious expression eased, and a fleeting grin crossed his face. 'Talking of miracles, Ellie's pregnant.'

Josh felt the knife twist a little more. What must it be like to know that your partner was carrying your child? To watch her body swell with the burgeoning life within her, to feel the early movements of your child, to wait anxiously for the great day, and then the moment itself when you first held your child in your arms——?

Josh felt a sharp prickling behind his eyes, and blinked. 'That's great, Mike,' he said gruffly, and the ache inside him grew a little more.

Mike handed him a small brochure. 'Here—you can see your ad, and sift through the others.'

Josh glanced at the little booklet in horrified surprise. 'I'm in here?'

Mike nodded. 'They didn't want to place your ad without your input, but I managed to persuade them.'

'Persuade Ellie, you mean.'

Mike grinned. Ellie still worked for the agency, and Josh suspected the lively little blonde of rather more input than Mike admitted to.

'It's—um—a rather off-beat ad,' Mike said with a touch of awkwardness, and Josh's heart sank.

'Off-beat?'

'Yeah. Um,' Mike shifted in his seat, 'Ellie—ah—worded it.'

Josh scanned the pages, passed over one which bore his name but not his description, and then came back to it, disbelief warring with faint hysteria.

'You jest. "Joshua, thirty, tall, dark and handsome,

single, doctor, witty, sexy eyes, luscious body''—dear God, I don't believe this—''excellent health, GSOH''—what the hell's that?'

'Good sense of humour.'

Josh snorted rudely. 'Oh, yeah? "GSOH, NS".' He quirked an eyebrow at his brother.

'Non-smoker.'

'Right. ''Likes children, animals, dining out, theatre''—this is rubbish. When do I dine out or go to the theatre? I never have time.'

'Would you like to?'

'I'd like to have time,' he said drily.

'Fine. Go on.'

'"Travel and anything physical".' He snorted again, and Mike chuckled. 'Lord, it gets worse. ''His only fault is modesty. He's looking for an intelligent, NS, educated woman with GSOH and kind heart for fun, laughter and possible lasting relationship.'' Oh, God, Mike, when I see Ellie I'll kill her!'

Mike grinned uncomfortably. 'That's why I told you she's pregnant. I know you wouldn't hurt a pregnant woman.'

Josh threw the booklet down in disgust. 'That is such claptrap! Anything physical, indeed—it sounds positively depraved!'

'You object to sex?'

'Of course I don't object to sex, but I don't expect to have to advertise for it!'

Mike glanced at his watch. 'Er—I have to go. I'm meeting Ellie for lunch. Shall I tell her you'll be in touch?'

'Tell her not to hold her breath,' Josh said drily.

'Um—right. Happy birthday, big brother.'

Josh watched his younger sibling almost flee from the flat they used to share, and sighed. 'Anything physical, for God's sake! I'll kill her.' He picked up the brochure again, and flicked idly through it, examining the other adverts.

His own stood out by miles. Nobody else was that outrageous. God only knows what sort of woman it would attract—he'd have to take an armed escort for his own safety! Throwing the booklet into the corner, he stomped into the kitchen, turned on the tap and started washing up. 'Luscious body, indeed. God, I'll kill that woman. No way—no way!'

It was three months before he gave in to Mike's and Ellie's persistent nagging and glanced through the newest brochure with ill-concealed bad grace. It was Thursday, the beginning of April, and he was off duty after a hectic and particularly bloody weekend. It would have been nice to go for a walk, but there was no one to go with.

There was never anyone to go anywhere with—or no one who appealed. Perhaps with the whole of London to choose from he was just too damn fussy. There was that staff nurse with the big chest and the pushy manner, but she spelled trouble with a capital T. The others were already married, engaged or heavily involved—or on the rebound. He didn't need that sort of aggravation. Instead he would spend the time proving to Ellie and Mike that the right woman didn't exist.

He flicked through the brochure, noticing his own ad with disgust, and finally got to the women's adverts. He scanned down them uninterestedly. They seemed to fall into two groups—the lonely misfits, and the raving nymphomaniacs. Certainly there was no one who appealed to him, he thought with what seemed horrifyingly like disappointment.

Then he turned the page, and his uninterested scanning came to a grinding, crashing halt on a single word.

Melissa.

He read the paragraph aloud slowly. '"Melissa, thirty-three, paediatric nurse, NS, GSOH, loves children and animals, looking for like-minded intelligent companion to share walks in the country and quiet nights by the fire."' He lowered the brochure and gazed sightlessly across the room. Walks in the country, and quiet nights by the fire. Yearning gripped him, and he glanced at the little paragraph again. There was no physical description, which was a point in her favour, at least. And there was her name. 'Melissa— Lissa.' He tasted the word on his tongue, and felt a sudden, unexpected stab of desire dart through him.

He hesitated for a second, then reached decisively for the phone. If he was going to do it, he might as well get on with it. At least if he made an effort it would get Mike and Ellie off his back for a while. Not that she would measure up, of course. . .

Ellie answered after two rings.

'It's me,' he told her bluntly. 'The guy with the luscious bod.'

She giggled deliciously. 'Sorry, Josh,' she said totally unrepentant. 'What can I do for you?'

'Um, there's a girl. . .' He floundered to a halt, unsure how to continue. Suddenly he felt rather foolish and terribly vulnerable, and he wished to God he'd never rung her.

'In our brochure? What's her name? I'll see what else I can tell you about her.'

'Liss——' He coughed and cleared his throat, then tried again. 'Melissa.'

'Ah. Actually, Josh, I was going to contact you because she's rung about you, too.'

'She has?' Josh was stunned.

'Uh-huh. She'd like to meet you. I interviewed her myself, and she's super. I think you'd be a brilliant match. Shall I give her your number?'

So she was curious about him, too? Interesting. 'She's not violent? Not a pervert or anything? It's just that the ad was a bit——'

Ellie giggled. 'It was just a bit of fun, Josh—and no, she's not at all weird. She's been with us for a few months now and she's quite safe. You won't need a bodyguard.'

'Why hasn't she found anyone?'

He could almost hear Ellie shrug. 'The same reason you haven't? I guess she's just fussy. She's had a few dates, but she hasn't seen anyone more than once yet. I get the feeling she knows what she wants. I just wish you did——'

'Tell me about her,' Josh asked, dragging Ellie back to the point and waiting in what felt suspiciously like suspense. He just knew he was going to be disillusioned.

'Right, let me check her file. . .it's just here,' Ellie said. There was a flurry of paper, and then she spoke again. 'She's about five feet five, fine bones but a little bit plump, perhaps, very pretty, hair like a shampoo advert—long, blonde, heavy—fabulous hair. She's got a terrific sense of humour, a lovely rich laugh, smoky grey eyes—lovely girl. Her husband was a bit of a toad, from what I can gather. She didn't talk much about him. They got divorced six years ago and she's been on her own ever since. She told me the sands of time were slipping by and it was now or never. She's older than you—does that worry you?'

'No. Women live longer anyway. The more practice she's had, the better cook she'll be.'

Ellie tutted disapprovingly. 'It's a good job I don't take you seriously. So, what do you think? Shall I give her your number and get her to contact you?'

Josh took a steadying breath. What was he agreeing

to, after all? One date, perhaps not even that. 'Yes—
yes, do that, Ellie. How's the baby coming on, by
the way?'

Her voice softened. 'Fine, thanks. I've had to buy
a complete new wardrobe.'

'Shame.'

'Isn't it?' She chuckled. 'I'll ring Melissa now—are
you at home this evening?'

'Yes—and almost every other one, except when I'm
on duty. I'll wait for Melissa to call.'

He cradled the phone and then found himself staring
at it, willing it to ring. Ridiculous. She probably
wouldn't even bother. Anyway, it would be hours
before Ellie got hold of her.

He was just stuffing shirts into the washing-machine
that evening when the phone jangled. He jumped,
stared at it, then lifted it. 'Hello? Josh Lancaster.'

Her voice was like honey. By the time he put the
phone down his heart was pounding, his jeans were
conspicuously tighter and he was shaking from head
to foot.

And he was meeting her the following evening.

CHAPTER ONE

MELISSA cradled the screaming child against her chest
and rocked her soothingly.

'Hush, sweetheart, it's all right. We'll soon make
you better. It's all right, Emily, it's all right. . .' She
crooned softly to the terrified toddler, and gradually
she felt the child's body relax a little. It was difficult
to hold her because of the burns that covered both
arms, but the poor little scrap was desperate for a
cuddle and Melissa simply couldn't bear her cries.

So she held her carefully, pressed her lips against
the soft golden curls, and murmured sweet nothings.
It couldn't take the pain away, but for a tiny child
such strange smells and sounds were nearly as bad as
the pain, and they needed reassurance as much as they
needed anything.

If only her mother could be here, but she was in ITU
now with second and third degree burns and smoke
inhalation from trying to rescue Emily's older brother.
A fireman had got the boy out the back way unhurt,
but the mother hadn't realised and had gone in the
front again, nearly losing her life.

The father was comforting his son, praying for his
wife and only too relieved to hand the baby over once
he was sure she would be all right.

Melissa wished she was as confident. Oh, sure, the
baby would live, but she needed pain relief fast, and
they had been so busy down on A and E that they
had sent her straight up for the paediatricians to deal
with on the ward.

So the paediatric SHO who had admitted Emily was

13

going to have to put in an intravenous line to replace
lost fluids, because the consultant, Andrew Barrett,
was away at a conference and his senior registrar had
left and the replacement didn't arrive until tomorrow.
A great pity, because the SHO was useless at finding
tiny veins. If only the new man had arrived. . .

She heard footsteps behind her, a firm, steady tread,
not loud but decisive. They reminded her of someone
else—someone she was struggling to forget. It was
probably a parent, someone looking for a child. She
looked up, a welcoming smile on her face, and her
breath jammed in her throat.

It couldn't be him—she was imagining it, conjuring
him out of thin air because of the stupid ache inside
that wouldn't go away——

'Hello, Melissa.'

She was speechless for a moment, still struggling
with the lump in her throat. Lord, he looked wonderful—even more devastating than she remembered. . .

She blinked, but he didn't go away. She swallowed
the lump. 'What—how did you—Josh, why are
you here?'

'Because I'm Barrett's new SR. I just came to
acquaint myself with the ward staff and routine before
tomorrow.'

Her mind scrambled to make sense of that. 'You're
going to be working here?' she said finally.

'Yes.' His lips lifted in a wry smile. 'Isn't coincidence
a wonderful thing?'

Emily whimpered, and he glanced down at the baby
in her arms. 'What have you got here?'

She dragged her befuddled mind back to her job.
'Burns—mum's in ITU. The rest of the family are
all right.'

'May I see?' He crouched beside her, his big knee
jutting against her leg, and an unforgotten fire shot

through her. His head was by her shoulder, the dark hair soft and thick. She remembered only too well how it felt, sifting through her fingers. . . . Lord, why was he here?

She watched as he turned back the towel that covered the child, and saw compassion as well as professional assessment in his eyes. His voice was soft, soothing the baby as he examined her with great care.

'She'll need a line in to replace her fluids—did she inhale any smoke, do you know?'

'Not much as far as they're aware. She's unharmed except for the arms and a small burn on one cheek. They're all first or minor second degree.'

He nodded. 'The most painful, but frankly the more it hurts the happier I am because of the level of damage. At least if it hurts it means her nerves are intact.' He turned one arm over very carefully, then laid it back down. 'She should heal without any scarring if she's lucky. She'll need a line in her leg, I think. Is the SR going to do it?'

She shook her head. 'No—he's gone, and the consultant's not back till tomorrow either. It's the SHO, I'm afraid.'

There must have been something in her voice, because Josh shot her a searching look and then gently squeezed the child's leg. 'Tiny veins—is he up to it? She's in shock, and her circulation's shutting down. It won't be easy.'

She let out a tiny sigh. 'There's no choice, is there?'

'There is—I'm here.'

'But you haven't started yet——'

'Stuff that. Where can I get a white coat?'

Melissa felt the tension draining out of her shoulders. 'In the office. There's a clean one hanging on the back of the door.'

'Are you all right holding her? I'll get someone else

to assist at this end, but I don't want to move her as she seems comfortable.'

Melissa nodded. 'Get Anna Long—she's the staff nurse on duty. She's got all the things ready. She's at the desk—the redhead.'

He straightened up and walked briskly over to the nursing station. She heard the murmur of his voice, and watched as Anna stared up at Josh for a second then fluttered into action. She couldn't blame the girl for her reaction to him. He just seemed to do that to women, herself included.

God knows she was no one to criticise anybody for falling under his spell. She had—and with indecent haste. How had he found her? She didn't believe in coincidence. He was here for a reason, and she was damn sure she was it. He must have been looking for her for nearly four months now, but he'd had precious little to go on. He hadn't even had her surname, just her Christian name, that was all. She had made sure he wouldn't be able to contact her. The agency? No. They'd promised not to give him any details.

How, then?'

God knows. Maybe it really was coincidence, although she doubted it. Hospitals were hotbeds of gossip. Everybody knew everybody else's business, so no doubt he had simply asked if anyone knew a Melissa.

She sighed. She knew she should have used a false name, then he wouldn't have traced her—because trace her he had, she was sure of that. Why else hadn't he been as surprised as she was when he walked on to the ward? Unless, of course, he really was indifferent to her. After all, it had been a very short fling, and several months ago. . .

She watched as he came out of the office, shrugging on the coat and walking towards her again, those

wonderful blue eyes searching her face, seeing
too much.

She schooled her expression while her heart thrashed
and pounded. Whatever his motives, he was here now
and, as far as her carefully laid plans went, that spelled
disaster. How could she hide? Not just herself, but the
rest—the most important thing?

As soon as she stood up he would see, and she knew
him well enough even after one weekend to realise he
would never give up then.

The child in her arms must have picked up her dread,
because she started to cry again. Taking a steadying
breath, Melissa turned her attention back to the little
one and forced herself to relax and focus on the child.

'It's all right, sweetheart. It'll soon be better,' she
crooned, and, rocking her tenderly, she soothed the
damp hair back from her forehead and gave the baby
an encouraging smile.

He was there now, on the edge of her vision, working
with Anna to prepare the site, heating the area over
the vein to distend it, putting a strap round her leg to
restrict the venous return. Amazingly a vein appeared,
tiny but just visible. His hands strong and yet gentle,
he grasped the child's ankle and quickly slipped
the cannula into the impossibly tiny vein with
ridiculous ease.

The baby screamed and wriggled, but he held her
firmly and Anna taped the tube down, connected up
the intravenous fluids and checked the morphine
syringe with Josh before he injected it slowly into
the tube.

Gradually, as the drug took effect, the little girl's
struggles subsided and she lay drowsily in Melissa's
arms, whimpering slightly.

'There, that wasn't so bad, was it?' he murmured to
the baby.

'Piece of cake—anyone would think you'd done it before,' Melissa said with a smile, and he looked up and met her eyes, his own crinkled at the edges.

'Just once or twice,' he agreed, then turned his attention back to the baby, who was still whimpering occasionally.

'Poor little scrap,' Josh said softly, his voice rich with compassion. 'Let's get her into bed and comfortable, and we'll discuss her management. Shall I take her?'

Without waiting for a reply he bent and scooped up the child, towel and all, and laid her in the empty cot that had been prepared for her. His big hand brushed tenderly over her brow, his eyes searching the burn on her cheek, and then he turned back to Melissa. 'Have you done a map of her burns?'

'No. We ought to do that now. Anna, have we got a chart?'

'Here.' Anna handed Melissa the clipboard from the end of the cot. It was made up with charts for drugs, vital signs and a body map on which to shade the area of her burns, in order to calculate the percentage of her body that had been affected. The drugs and fluids she would be given would be calculated from that area and from her weight.

'Right, let's look at her,' Josh said. 'Melissa, could you shade the map?'

There was no alternative but to stand up and join him at the cotside. As she did so she saw his eyes flick down her body, hesitate, then focus with a slight frown on her midsection.

Then, almost in slow motion, he dragged his eyes back up to hers.

'Lissa?' His voice sounded scrapy and unused, and his eyes, when she dared to look at them, were wary.

'Could we talk about this another time?' she said in

an undertone, and turned her attention to the baby. 'Right arm—all of forearm, both sides, back of hand and fingers, not palm. Agree?'

She was conscious of Josh's eyes on her until he dragged them away and forced his attention to the child. 'Yes. Left arm the same, forearm only below the elbow, not all of the underside. We'll have to watch for swelling—she might need an incision through the burns in one or other arm to relieve pressure if her circulation becomes compromised or a joint gets restricted. Hopefully it won't. As for her face, it's very superficial and should heal without scarring.'

He listened to her chest, observed her breathing for a minute and then nodded. 'So far so good. We'll have to watch her for any later signs of smoke inhalation— bronchiolitis, pulmonary oedema, obstruction from swelling. It could come on at any time, although she sounds clear now. I want her nappies weighed and her fluids monitored. She can have drinks ad lib, but measured, please, and we'll start her with one and a half units of plasma over the first twenty-four hours, assuming she weighs about fifteen kilos. Has anybody weighed her?'

Anna shook her head. 'No—not that I know of. Melissa?'

'No, but I should say that's about right. I calculate her burn area at around nine per cent, of mainly first and some second degree superficial burns. Do you agree?'

Josh scanned the little patient again and nodded. 'Yes. Because she's so young it's more serious, and also because of the small burn on her face, but I don't think she'll be a problem. We ought to remove the blisters, cover the burns with a non-adherent occlusive dressing and smother it in Flamazine twice a day to prevent bacterial infection, but you'll have to watch for swelling more often than that—check the dressings every two hours at first for the next couple of days. I don't want her circulation cut off while we all doze off on her.'

His grin was infectious, and Anna laughed, a soft, flirtatious sound that made Melissa bristle—absurdly, because she had no right to Josh, in fact didn't want a right to him or anything to do with him. . .except the one thing that was making it hard for both of them to concentrate at the moment.

'I'll get the dressings sorted out—shall we do it in here?' Anna was saying.

'Good idea—you go and find what we need and Sister Shaw and I will discuss the case a little further.'

Melissa opened her mouth to comment, but there was nothing to say.

Anna was gone, and she was alone with Josh, in a yawning void that seemed impossible to fill.

She fiddled with the chart for a moment, but then found it gently but firmly taken out of her hands.

'Lissa?'

Nobody else had ever called her that, and it made her tremble, deep down inside, so that her voice wasn't as steady as she might have liked. She was calm, though. There was a fatalistic sense of inevitability about this conversation. 'Yes?' she said.

Strong fingers tilted her chin, making her meet his eyes. They were bluer even than she remembered, and she had the distinct feeling they would see straight through any attempt to lie.

'You're pregnant,' he stated softly.

'Yes,' she said again. She could hardly deny it.

'When's the baby due?'

She hesitated, but those blue eyes narrowed slightly and the fingers tightened oh, so slightly on her chin.

'When, Melissa?'

'December.'

'When in December?'

There was no point in lying. She had decided to tell him anyway. He might as well know now. 'The twenty-ninth.'

Slowly, ever so slowly, his hand fell away. 'Well, there's a thing. Thirty-eight weeks from the end of December is the second weekend in April, give or take the odd day. What an extraordinary coincidence.'

'It seems to be the day for them,' she replied. She said nothing else. There was nothing to be said, and anyway Anna came bustling back into the room pushing a trolley piled to the sky with dressings, creams, saline and clothes for Emily.

'Do you want to do the dressings, Melissa? I haven't done burns for ages.'

Melissa dragged her eyes away from the accusing blue of Josh's magnetic glare.

'Sure—they just need covering loosely to prevent infection and stop her damaging the healing skin. Was there anything you wanted to add, Dr Lancaster?'

'Plenty, but it'll keep,' he muttered, and, turning on his heel, he stalked over to the work station and started running through the computer.

'Phew—did you get up his nose or something?' Anna asked, staring after him in surprise.

'Um—we know each other,' Melissa said weakly.

'Fancy falling out with a hunk like that—what a waste!'

Melissa glared at her staff nurse, and with a muttered apology the girl subsided and became quietly efficient, to Melissa's enormous relief. It was bad enough dealing with the shock of Josh's sudden reappearance in her life, without having to fend off Anna's insatiable curiosity.

She managed to avoid being alone with him through-

out the rest of that very busy day. It was hot, the
August sun beating down on the windows so that they
needed the blinds drawn to keep the children cool.

The children in plasters and traction were bored and
irritable, itchy under their casts and generally a pain
in the neck. She entertained them whenever she had
time, but they had been bottled up with a teacher all
morning, the play assistant was with the little ones,
and, frankly, as ward sister she was too busy to play,
although she would have loved to.

One in particular, a boy called Simon, was in for
long-term orthopaedic work on his smashed legs, and
although he was supposed to be non-weight-bearing
kept getting out of bed and limping about in his casts.
He was frustrated, in pain and bored absolutely rigid,
and he was a real challenge to the patience of the
nursing staff.

That particular afternoon he was too much for
Melissa's patience, and she told him off roundly and
sent him back to bed, her usual gentle good-humour
sorely lacking.

It was Josh's fault, she knew, but she felt guilty for
being so hard on Simon and went back to apologise.

'I know you've had enough. It must be awful. I'm
sorry I was so ratty with you earlier,' she said quietly
as she gave him his drugs.

'That's OK,' he said with a grin. 'I know you get
fed up with me. I'm a pain. Still, maybe soon I'll be
able to get up and walk and things.'

'Not if you don't follow the doctor's orders,' Melissa
warned. 'We could always put you back in traction.'

He crossed his two index fingers and held them up
towards her, pretending to cower on the bed. 'It's a
witch! Aaagh, lads, take cover!'

She grinned in defeat, gave him a playful smack on
the hand and left them to it. Little horrors.

When the little toddler Emily began to show signs of respiratory distress by three o'clock, Melissa was forced to choose between an SHO she really didn't trust, or the one man in the world she really didn't want to see.

For Emily's sake there was no choice. She picked up the phone and asked the switchboard to page Josh. He was apparently moving into the doctors' residence and had told her he would be around if he was needed.

He arrived promptly. 'Problems?' he asked.

'Yes—Emily. I'm sorry to disturb you while you're settling in, but she's showing signs of respiratory distress. I've put her in an oxygen tent with a humidifier, and that's helped a little.'

Josh nodded. 'We'll check her blood gases—can you help me get a sample of arterial blood from her?'

'Of course—I'll get the things.'

She went into the stores and took a steadying breath. Damn, why did he still turn her to mush with that soft, deep voice? There was something almost intimate about standing head to head and talking quietly, even if it was about a patient. It reminded her of dancing with him, of dining by candlelight or walking arm in arm through the woods—or lying side by side sharing the same pillow in the aftermath of loving——

'I think we might have to intubate her—we'll see what the results come up with. I'd rather not wait until she's too distressed.' He was lounging in the doorway of the stores, looking altogether too attractive for her peace of mind. She had enough to deal with, for heaven's sake, without her hormones getting in the way!

She tried to concentrate on the job. He wanted to intubate her now—or after the results? Oh, hell. . . 'OK,' she said, not sure what she was agreeing with, and closed her eyes. Damn, her voice was as scratchy as an old woollen vest. She gritted her teeth, snatched down the necessary supplies and turned, cannoning into his chest.

'Easy,' he murmured, catching her elbows to steady her while the packs rained on to the floor around them.

'I thought you'd gone,' she muttered crossly, bending to pick up the supplies. 'If you hadn't crept up behind me——'

'Sorry. Here.' He handed her the last pack and she pushed past him, conscious of his eyes and the touch of his hand against hers, scorching her skin. She almost expected it to blister like Emily's.

They took her nappy off and went into the femoral artery in her groin for the blood gases sample. Predictably the little girl screamed and tried to wriggle, but Melissa held her firmly until the procedure was over, then cuddled her, crooning softly to her while Josh filled bottles and wrote up lab request forms.

'We'll do a red cell count as well to check she hasn't lost too much plasma. If it comes back concentrated we'll give her another unit over the next twenty-four hours.' He flicked through the notes, pursed his lips and glanced at the little child on Melissa's lap. 'Any news of the mother?'

'Nothing new. The father's down there with her. They've got a relative looking after the older boy.'

Josh chewed the end of his pen thoughtfully, then stuck it back in his top pocket and hung the clipboard back on the end of the cot. 'I'd like to talk to the father about her when we get the results of the blood gases. I'll get the lab to page me with them, then I'll come up. Perhaps we can go down to ITU and see him there if he doesn't want to leave his wife.'

Melissa nodded. 'OK. I'll contact you if her condition deteriorates. Will you still be around?'

'Yes, I'll be in my room.'

He turned on his heel and left, and Melissa let her breath out in a quiet sigh and tucked Emily back in her cot. She clung to Melissa, and she had to pry the sore little fingers carefully away from her hands.

'I'll be back in a minute,' she promised, but the baby still cried.

Melissa, her eyes filling, went out to the work station, called the lab porter to take the samples down for immediate analysis and then went to quell a riot in the older children's room.

'Hey, you lot!' she called over the din. 'It's time for children's TV. Shall I turn it on?'

And thank God for the electronic babysitter, she thought as she left them settling down in front of a cartoon.

She had a headache coming on, and in the background she could hear little Emily crying sporadically in her cot.

She wasn't due for any more pain relief for another hour, but Melissa thought it wasn't pain so much as distress that was making her cry. The result of her blood gases had come back and Josh had phoned them through. Fortunately she wouldn't need to be intubated, which meant she could have something to eat now.

Melissa checked the ward quickly, took a water jug away from a pre-op patient who had been given it by mistake, chastised the junior responsible and shut herself into the little room with the miserable toddler and a jar of chocolate pudding.

'Come here, sweetheart—let's give you some pudding. Are you hungry?' she murmured, and, scooping the little one on to her lap, she snuggled her down with the oxygen playing on her face, dipped the tip of the spoon in the chocolate goo and held it to Emily's lips. 'Here, darling, try this. Mmm—is that lovely? More?'

The little one nodded, her eyes like saucers, and Melissa coaxed and tempted her through the whole jar. Towards the end her eyes began to droop, so Melissa began to hum softly to her, watching as the lids slid shut and the child's breathing eased into the peaceful rhythm of sleep.

She was so engrossed that she hardly noticed the door opening. It shut again just as quietly, and she put the spoon down and carefully eased the sleeping baby back into the cot.

Only then did she look up. He was standing just inside the door, watching her with a strange expression on his face, and for some reason it filled her with a mixture of security and foreboding.

'OK?' he asked softly.

She nodded. 'How was her blood count?'

'Her red cells are a bit concentrated. We'll continue with the plasma for another twenty-four hours.'

Melissa tucked the soft cotton blanket round the baby, rearranged the oxygen drape and straightened up.

'Good. I've managed to get her to eat something at last.'

Josh stood by the cot, that strange look on his face. 'I've contacted Emily's father,' he murmured. 'He's coming up at five-thirty. His wife's stable for now.'

'Thank God for that. I imagine the situation could change?'

He nodded. 'Smoke inhalation—she may get more severe respiratory problems, but the chest man seems hopeful that she won't. How's the babe's breathing?'

'Easier with the oxygen. I think it's as bad as it'll get.'

'Good.' He eyed her thoughtfully. 'Melissa, we need to talk.'

Her heart thumped. She had wondered how long she'd get away with it. Now she knew. 'There's nothing to talk about,' she told him as firmly as she could manage.

Josh thought otherwise, evidently.

'Were you going to tell me?' he asked, and the bitterness in his voice hurt her more than she would have believed possible.

She sighed. 'Yes—eventually.'

'So you're not denying that it's mine?'

She looked up again, into those stormy, blazing blue eyes. 'Under the circumstances that would be rather silly, wouldn't it? Anyway, I never intended to keep it a secret.'

He gave a restrained but expressive snort. 'Big of you.'

Lord, he sounded angry. Not surprising, really. She would be. Still, she had to deflect him. Men weren't nearly so territorial about children as women—only as a matter of pride. Once it arrived and was smelly and messy, he'd soon lose interest, if he didn't before.

She had to make a stand. Resting her hands on the end of the cot, she forced herself to look into his eyes. It was a mistake. They were beautiful, blazing mad and very, very determined. 'Joshua, it's my baby,' she told him quietly. 'Not yours. Mine. You were merely there at the time.'

'Merely there—my God, woman, what do you mean I was merely there? I won't be brushed aside as a mere biological necessity!'

'You should have thought of that when you took me to bed,' she said sharply. 'If you were that bothered about it, you should have made damn sure it didn't happen!'

'But you said you were on the Pill!'

She shook her head. 'No. I said I'd seen a doctor.

It was hardly a lie—I was looking at one at the time.'

Contempt clouded his eyes. 'That is so unbelievably irresponsible. How the hell did you imagine you were going to look after it—or were you after me for a meal ticket for life? Is that it? Find someone with a good potential income and slap a paternity suit on the poor stupid bastard?'

Her knuckles whitened on the end of the cot. 'I have an income—a private income—and a home. I thought of all that before——'

She broke off. Damn, she had said too much. Appalled, she watched realisation dawn in his eyes.

Anger tightened his mouth, drawing a white line round his lips and setting his jaw. 'Damn you, you used me as a stud!' he said, his voice coloured with horrified disbelief. 'You deliberately set out to seduce me in order to get pregnant, didn't you?'

She said nothing. What could she say?

He grabbed her, yanking her up against his chest. 'Didn't you?' he growled.

She met his eyes, blazing with fury and hurt, and hated herself.

'Yes,' she told him quietly. 'I did.'

He dropped her as if she was poisonous, and stepped back. 'Well, get this, Melissa. There's no way your little plan is going to work, because I intend to be involved every single step of the way, from now onwards for the next thirty or forty years. You can forget any ideas you had about bringing it up alone, do you understand? Because that's my baby!'

There was a discreet cough behind them.

'Excuse me—Melissa?'

She looked up, dazed, and could have wept. Anna, working a split shift, had come back on duty and was standing in the doorway, a carefully schooled expression on her face—and a stranger in tow.

'Um—this is Emily's father, Mr Gordon,' she said hesitantly, looking from one to the other.

Melissa could have screamed. 'We'll talk later,' she said to Josh.

'Too damn right,' he growled under his breath, and, turning on his heel, he pushed past Anna and held out his hand to Emily's father. 'Hello, Mr Gordon, I'm Dr Lancaster. I'm in charge of your daughter's case. Would you come with me?'

Anna took one look at Melissa's face and fled without a word.

CHAPTER TWO

Josh sat down heavily on the bed and stared sightlessly out of the window of the tatty little hospital room that was home for however long.

There was a brick wall opposite, but he didn't see it. All he could see were Melissa's beautiful, smoke-hued, lying eyes and the soft swell of her body as it cradled her child.

His child.

'Mine,' he said aloud. A pang of something violent and paternal stabbed him and his fists bunched in the over-washed bedspread.

'Melissa.'

He used her name as a curse, his voice a harsh rasp in the quiet room.

He couldn't bring himself to call her Lissa. That was a name for a special time, a time when he had taken her in his arms and fallen headlong in love—a time that was all just a tissue of lies.

He had thought they were lovers. Instead, he was just a carefully chosen stud.

'Stud.' He said the word aloud, trying it for size. It left a vile taste in his mouth. How could he have been so gullible? Surely he should have seen through her? Scheming witch.

Why him, for God's sake? What about some other sucker who didn't give a damn about kids? Why choose someone whose whole life revolved around them, someone to whom their health and happiness was more important than anything else?

And why now, when he had spent weeks anticipating

30

their next meeting, winning her round, wooing her—damn it, he had even fantasised about their getting married and her having his child, and then when he had seen she was pregnant and realised it was his the surge of joy he had felt had stunned him.

Not as much, though, as the realisation that she had used him as a stud——

He shrugged to his feet, pacing in the tiny room, frustrated because there was no space to rant.

Changing quickly into jeans and a T-shirt, he grabbed a sweatshirt from his case and his wallet from the top of the single chest of drawers; pocketing his keys, he left the claustrophobically small room, striding down the corridor towards the car park, his long legs burning off the distance in seconds. At the end of the corridor he hesitated, swung towards the main part of the hospital and rapidly made his way to the switchboard office.

'I need to contact Melissa Shaw at home,' he told the telephonist, lying fluently. 'She's not answering, so I thought I'd drop a note in her door so she rings me as soon as she's back—I need to see her about a baby.' Well, that part wasn't a lie.

The telephonist regarded him suspiciously. 'Who are you, please?'

'Dr Lancaster—Josh,' he said, tacking on a disarming grin as an afterthought. 'Andrew Barrett's new SR. Pleased to meet you——' he peered at the badge on her chest '—Jinny.' His eyes flicked back to her face. 'It really is very important,' he added in his most serious caring-doctor voice. She buckled, as he had known she would. He felt a little twinge of guilt, but suppressed it. This was important.

'I suppose—under the circumstances it would be all right. . .' She flicked through a card index and jotted something down, handing it to him. 'Here's her address—Holly Cottage, Mill Common, Laxford. She usually leaves her answerphone on, though.'

Josh grinned again. 'Maybe she was in the bath or vacuuming or something. Thanks.' He winked, turned on his heel and headed for the door.

Right, Melissa, he thought, all trace of a smile gone from his face. Time for our little chat.

She wasn't surprised when a car pulled on to her drive and Josh unfolded himself from behind the wheel. In fact, if he hadn't turned up she would have been more surprised.

That was why she had gone right through the house with the vacuum cleaner and tidied it from end to end.

She had just thrown the last few pots and pans in the dishwasher and tugged on the most figure-skimming of her new maternity dresses when she heard the car. Taking a steadying breath and wiping her suddenly damp palms on the soft cotton knit of her dress, she opened the door and watched as he crossed the lawn, ducking under the sweeping branches of the apple tree and almost tripping over the cat.

He stroked it automatically and Calico, the faithless feline, purred and squawked and wound himself against Josh's legs. Josh straightened up and looked at her.

'Don't tell me—another coincidence. You know someone next door,' she said drily.

'Hardly. We have unfinished business,' Josh told her, his voice deceptively mild.

She snorted. 'So you say.'

'I do. You want me to go over it all again?'

She bit her lip to trap the retort. After all, she did owe him at least an explanation. 'You'd better come in. It's sufficient that our affair is broadcast all over the hospital, without its being telegraphed to the whole of Mill Common as well.'

She picked up the cat out of jealousy, dropped him on the kitchen floor by his food bowl and shut the door on him firmly.

Then she turned back to find Josh ambling round her room, picking things up and examining them with idle curiosity before setting them down and moving on to the next. It infuriated her.

'Do you suppose you could stick to the matter in question, instead of cataloguing my possessions and interfering with my ornaments?' she snapped.

He turned, one eyebrow raised quizzically. 'Touchy, aren't you? Is that a symptom of a guilty conscience?' He eyed her as the blush rose on her throat. 'I'll give you the benefit of the doubt and say it is. Good. That's your first redeeming feature. Probably the only one. I doubt I'll find another.'

The harshness of his tone brought tears to her eyes. She blinked and lowered her head, unwilling to let him see how his words affected her. 'Josh, please listen to my side before you judge me,' she said quietly.

'By all means,' he said, lowering himself into her corner of the sofa and stretching out, 'but do me a favour and save the tears. I'm really not that gullible.'

She lifted her head, a swift retort on her lips, but he cut her off before she opened her mouth.

'A cup of tea would be nice.'

She snorted. 'Tough. Since you weren't invited, you can hardly complain about the standard of service.'

His mouth tightened. 'I didn't get us into this mess, you did, so don't give me a hard time because I try and be civilised about it! What would you rather I did, take you to court for custody?'

His words hung, frozen, in the silence.

After an endless moment she turned away. 'I'll make some tea.'

'Sensible girl,' he murmured behind her back, and she went into the kitchen, shut the door and sagged back against it.

'Cally, what am I going to do about him?' she asked the cat in a desperate, miserable undertone.

Calico squawked and rubbed himself against her legs, then looked at the door and squawked again.

'No. Faithless wretch.'

He sat down patiently and watched her as she filled the kettle and washed two of the mugs from the dishwasher, then made the tea. Knowing it would be impossible for her to get past him into the room, he waited patiently until she opened the door and then darted through, running to Josh and leaping lightly on to his lap.

Serve him right, Melissa thought spitefully. Demanding, horrid cat—he'd sink his claws into Josh's leg in a minute and all hell would break loose.

However, it didn't. Josh just stroked him with a gentle touch Melissa remembered so very, very well, and the cat collapsed in delight, kneading and dribbling and purring his head off. Melissa knew how he felt.

'Wretched cat—he'll drool all over you,' she flannelled, unable to drag her eyes away from that sure, caressing hand.

'He's fine. Don't worry about him; I'm used to cats.' A tinge of sarcasm entered his tone. 'I like children and animals, remember.'

She flushed, put his tea down beside him and headed for the only chair, tucking her feet under her bottom and curling up defensively, her mug cradled between her hands.

He sipped his tea, eyeing her assessingly over the rim as he absently scratched the cat's ears, then when the silence was almost unbearable he put the mug down and sighed.

'So, let's have it. What made you think you could find a stud, get laid and then bring up the little bastard on your own?'

His harsh words shocked her. 'Don't!' she protested softly. 'It wasn't like that, Josh. Don't cheapen it!'

'What? Our dirty weekend?'

He almost spat the words at her, and she recoiled, hurt at his description of what to her had been the most moving and beautiful time of her life. It had all happened too fast to call it love, but his humour and tenderness, and the gentle yet burning passion that had flared between them, had meant more to her than she could have imagined or dreamed. That was why she had walked away before it was too late, only it had been, of course—much too late. . .

'It wasn't dirty,' she said quietly.

'It wasn't exactly honest, either,' he countered. 'You lied, sweetheart. You never wanted a companion for walks in the woods and quiet evenings by the fire. You wanted a stud, a living, breathing sperm bank, and that's exactly what you set out to get. What we haven't yet established to my satisfaction is why.'

She swirled her tea, staring down into its murky depths with unwarranted concentration. He was right, of course. That was exactly what she had set out to do. The fact that she had changed her mind about using him once she realised the sort of person he was was neither here nor there, because she had already been pregnant. How was she to know it would be so quick? She had expected it would take months, years even, with her problematic history.

Observing his reaction, she didn't suppose that the reason why she'd done it would cut any ice with him, but she owed him at least the benefit of an explanation.

But where could she begin? Unfortunately the answer wasn't to be found in the tea leaves—particularly not as she used tea bags.

She set the mug down with a little thump on the table beside her, wound her fingers together to steady them and looked up at him.

'What do you know about endometriosis?'

A quick frown creased his brow. 'Endometriosis? In simple terms it means the lining of the womb is growing in the wrong place, either in the wall of the womb itself or in the abdomen, very occasionally in other sites. It can cause painful, heavy periods, infertility, painful intercourse. Modern drugs can suppress it in certain cases, but usually the most effective cure is hysterectomy. Sometimes it can be cured by pregnancy——' He broke off, searching her face as if he was looking for an answer, then his shoulders sagged and he shook his head. 'Is that why?' he said quietly. 'Have you got endometriosis?'

She nodded. 'Yes—with all of the above, and more. I was flooding every month, which meant I was getting desperately anaemic, I was in almost constant pain, my marriage had fallen apart because of the threat of infertility and the absence of a sex life—you name it, I had it. I wouldn't take time off sick, but I wasn't always really fit for work. Then I went to Jo Carter, one of the part-time gynae doctors here who runs the fertility clinic, and asked her what the future held for me.'

'And she told you to get pregnant as a cure.'

Melissa shook her head. 'No. She told me that she could treat the symptoms, but the only cure would be a hysterectomy. If I wanted a child, my time was running out, very fast.'

Josh regarded her steadily, and she wasn't sure but she thought some of the hostility had gone out of his eyes. 'So why not go the usual route and find a husband?'

'Because it would have been hypocritical, and anyway, there wasn't time.'

He laughed—a humourless, chilling sound. 'So instead of being hypocritical you lied. I must say your moral distinction leaves a great deal to be desired.'

She hugged her knees, feeling very vulnerable. It was hopeless; she would never convince him. 'I didn't—I don't—want a husband. It wasn't fair to trap a man under false pretences, just because I wanted a child.'

'And you think it was fair to deceive me into getting you pregnant? Hell's teeth, Lissa!'

His use of the pet name shocked them both into silence. She watched as the fight drained out of him, and he stabbed his hands through his hair. 'How could you? How could you sleep with me, say all those things to me, knowing you didn't mean any of it?'

She opened her mouth to deny it, but then thought better of it. It wasn't fair to give him any hope. Their relationship—and they would have one, because of the baby—was doomed to failure on a personal level. Her husband had seen to that. She would never be able to trust anyone again with her feelings. That was why she had broken all contact with Josh, because she sensed his involvement was deepening and she knew it wasn't fair.

Only it had been too late. He wanted to know how she could have slept with him and said all the things she'd said without meaning it. She almost laughed, because she had meant everything she had said, and as for sleeping with him, making love with him, it had been only too easy.

She made herself look him in the eye. 'I once heard someone say, "Women need a reason to have sex. Men just need a place." Well, I had a reason. All we needed was a place, and you obligingly provided that. Actually making love with you wasn't a problem. You're good. For the first time in my life I found I actually enjoyed it.'

He made a rude noise, obviously embarrassed by her compliment. 'So much for the painful intercourse.'

She looked down, unable to bear the derision in his eyes. 'It wasn't, with you.'

He snorted. 'Pity. It might have made you think a bit about what you were doing.'

'I did think!' she protested. 'I thought long and hard about it, but what was I supposed to do? Ask you to give me a baby?'

'At least it would have been honest, instead of that travesty of emotion we played out!'

Tears filled her eyes. She couldn't tell him the truth—it would make her too vulnerable—but she could apologise. At least her remorse was genuine, she thought sadly. 'I'm sorry I used you. I had no idea I would conceive so quickly, and if I hadn't I wouldn't have contacted you again. I'd already decided it wasn't morally acceptable, but it was too late. I was already pregnant.'

'You really expect me to believe you'd thought better of it? If that was the case, why hadn't you contacted me to tell me about the baby?'

'Because I didn't want you thinking I was after a meal ticket!' she yelled, her control ragged. 'Anyway, if you were so damn worried about it you should have used a condom!'

'About half a dozen, if my memory serves me correctly,' he said drily, and her cheeks flooded with colour. 'Yes, that's right, blush. I wonder which occasion it was, exactly, that brought about the life of our child? The first time, that Saturday evening, after our second date—you held back quite well there. What was wrong with the first date? Checking me out, were you?'

She felt her colour heighten again, and he made a sound of disgust.

'So, was it on Saturday evening, that very first time, or later—not very much later, if I recall,' he went on, his voice low and roughened, husky, tormenting her senses, 'because you wouldn't let me go and our bodies didn't even separate before lust overcame us again— was it then, I wonder, the second time?'

Heat flooded her body as she recalled her behaviour, clinging to him, loving the feel of his body, heavy against her; she remembered her astonishment as she had felt him grow again inside her, quickening to life again before the aftershocks had even died away, and then the tender, powerful intimacy of his lovemaking, the coiled strength, the gentleness, the shattering need that rose in her and swamped her—she buried her face in her hands, overwhelmed by the force of the memories.

'Stop it, Josh, for God's sake!' she whispered in desperation.

'Why? Was it so bad you can't bear to remember it? Or so good that you regret letting it go?' He went on relentlessly. 'Then we woke in the night and made love—sorry, had sex—again, then again in the shower, then again that Sunday night, then again in the morning just before you left. Six times, I believe I'm right in saying. Does that tie up with your memory——?'

'Stop it!' she screamed, covering her ears to shut out the endless tally of their loving. 'For pity's sake, Josh, stop. . .'

A sob rose in her throat, and, scrambling to her feet, she ran upstairs and into her bedroom, slamming the door before sinking down on the bed, the bitter tears scalding her cheeks as they fell.

After all the tender words he had spoken, the gentleness, the loving, that he could talk about it like that, and hate her so much—it tore her apart.

Turning her face into the pillow to muffle the sobs, she wept as though her heart was breaking.

Finally her emotion drained away, leaving her exhausted and empty. Scrubbing the tears from her cheeks, she pushed herself up and blinked, only to see Josh standing by the door, his face a tortured mask.

'Lissa, why?' he asked, his voice like sandpaper. 'Why me?'

She lifted her hands in a helpless gesture, then let them fall. She could give him that, at least.

'Because it needed to be someone I could respect, someone the baby could have pride in; someone who could be loved, so I could give the child the love it deserved. I couldn't guarantee you'd care about your baby, could I? So I had to be able to, knowing it was a part of you. I couldn't do that if I'd despised or disliked you.' She sniffed and looked round for a tissue. He was there first with a handful, and pressed them into her hand. She blew her nose, sniffed again and ran her hand back through the tangled mess of her hair.

'I'm really, truly sorry I hurt you,' she whispered brokenly. 'I didn't want to. That's why I went. Please don't hate me, Josh. I was desperate. I've wanted a child since I was about eighteen. I'm thirty-four now, and there's no time left. You were literally my last chance.'

The tears she'd thought were finished welled again, and to her surprise Josh sat down beside her, wrapped his arms around her and cradled her tenderly against his chest.

'Hush, Lissa. Don't cry any more. We'll sort something out.'

She pushed away from him. 'There's nothing to sort

out! I'm fine! I've got everything under control. Once
the baby's born we'll sort out visitation rights and that
sort of thing——'

'I'm not talking about visitation rights,' he murmured. 'I'm talking about you.'

'What about me?' she said desperately. 'I'm OK!'

'Are you? You look pretty washed out to me.'

'I'm tired——'

'I can see that. Have you eaten?'

She shook her head. 'I'm not hungry.'

'Rubbish. You have a warm bath, I'll knock you up
some supper and then you need an early night. You've
got fifteen minutes.'

She listened to his footsteps going down the stairs,
and sat there on the edge of the bed wondering about
his change of heart. Had he forgiven her? Or was he
just being civilised?

Oh, lord, his arms had felt so good around her. She
missed the feel of them—though how she could when
she'd never had time for him to become a habit. . .
Her eyes filled again, and with an impatient sniff she
stood up, marched into the bathroom and ran a bath.
Peeling off the dress and hanging it on the back of the
door, she slipped into the warm water, lay back and
stared at the ceiling. She could hear him in the kitchen,
banging about and muttering. God knows what he'd
find to feed her on. He'd probably tell her off about
that as well.

Right now she didn't care. The water felt wonderful.
She slid right down into it with a sigh, and let her
heavy, aching eyelids drift down. . .

Josh poked around in her fridge and came up with not
a lot. Damn fool woman, how did she think she could
take care of herself while she was pregnant with this
kind of housekeeping? In the end he found eggs, a

scrap of cheese and some reasonably fresh bread. An omelette was just about within his culinary capacity, so he found a pan in the dishwasher, scrubbed it out and put it on the hob to heat while he looked for dishwasher powder to put the machine on.

Nothing. She had run out of simply everything!

He found the last dribble of oil in a bottle to fry her omelette, grated the cheese into the egg mixture and poured it into the pan. While it cooked he filled the kettle for another cup of tea, sliced the ancient bread and put the nosy cat back on the floor.

He miaowed indignantly, but Josh was unrepentant. Cats on the worktop, especially around pregnant women, were a very bad idea. He washed his hands, elbowed the cat off the worktop again and watched as he stalked out of the catflap, disgusted.

Calico had his good points, Josh conceded. At least Melissa had a companion, although he wasn't much of a guard dog. Perhaps she should have a puppy—or, better yet, a human guard dog. Him, for instance.

God knows she needed looking after.

He didn't know why, but the woman tugged at his heartstrings. Even after all she had done, still there was something about her that tore at him—and it was nothing to do with the ache in his body from the memory of their lovemaking.

He shouldn't have called it sex. That had hurt her, because it had been lovemaking, he knew that. He had been reacting out of anger and pain, but deep down he knew that she wasn't lying about that.

Still, she didn't want him, and for some reason that hurt worse than anything else she had done.

The omelette was cooked, so he slid it out of the pan, put it under a low grill to keep warm and went upstairs to the bathroom door.

'Lissa?' There was no reply so he tapped, gently at first and then more firmly, concern nagging at him. Was she all right? When there was still no reply he tried the door, found it open and went in, his heart hammering.

She was fine, just asleep, her hair floating in the bath around her shoulders, her lashes black against her pale, tear-stained cheeks. As he looked at her the sigh of relief lodged in his throat. Her chest was rising and falling slowly with her even breathing, the soft globes of her pale breasts lapped gently by the water. Her hands rested on the smooth curve of her abdomen, cradling his child, and desire and yearning stabbed through him like white-hot needles.

He dragged his eyes away, ashamed at watching her while she slept, but, dear God, she was so lovely—even lovelier now than before, if that was possible.

He crouched beside the bath and shook her shoulder gently. 'Lissa? Wake up, sweetheart.'

Her lashes fluttered and she opened her eyes drowsily. 'Josh?' she murmured, and then sat up with a little scream and a flurry of water, her arms wrapped firmly across her breasts. 'What are you doing in here? Get out!'

'You fell asleep,' he told her, fixing his eyes on her face with sheer effort of will. 'I was worried about you. Come on, out you get. Your supper's ready.'

He put her towel within reach, turned on his heel and made himself walk out. A few minutes later she came down to the kitchen, her hair wrapped in a towel, her body swathed in a huge towelling robe that did nothing to diminish her loveliness, and fell on her omelette as if she hadn't eaten for weeks.

He stayed just long enough to give her a second cup

of tea, then left, forcing himself to concentrate on the road instead of the image of her gently swollen body that was burned into his mind.

That image kept him awake all night.

Little Emily was lying quietly in her cot when Melissa arrived on the ward. She had apparently had a fairly comfortable night, but she had refused all food, which was worrying because patients with burns needed to eat since the metabolism speeded up after such injuries and so the system needed more to sustain it. Melissa decided to try to get some food into her as soon as she had a minute.

There were other admissions: a seven-year-old boy with a nasty open fracture of the left forearm that had been reduced under anaesthetic; a ten-year-old girl with convulsions that had come on without warning or any prior history; and a six-year-old boy with a perforated appendix who had been operated on as an emergency during the night. He was in a poor condition with symptoms of peritonitis, and he was being specialled by a qualified nurse.

Otherwise the patients were as the previous day, with some discharges and new admissions under the ENT and ophthalmic surgeons. That was modern paediatrics, though. Kids in and out like fiddlers' elbows, with the average stay about twenty-four hours. It got through the clinical work, but made nursing more of a challenge.

How could you build a relationship with a child and earn his trust when he only saw you once or twice before you went off duty and someone else had to start all over again?

Thank God for mothers, Melissa thought fervently, smiling at one who was cradling her sleepy child on her knee. He had had a premed and was very drowsy, snuggled up comfortably with his head on his mother's heart.

Melissa wondered how Emily's mother was, and if she would live to hold her little girl like that again.

She did a quick ward round, checked on the new patients and went in to Emily with another jar of baby food. She no longer needed the oxygen tent all the time, and so was able to see people coming and going. When Melissa entered the room Emily turned towards her and held out a little bandaged hand.

'Hello, sweetheart,' Melissa said softly to the little girl, and she lifted her arms up and began to cry.

Melissa couldn't resist her plea. With a murmured word of consolation she lifted the little girl out of the cot and settled on the easy chair with her on her lap, the oxygen tent draped around them. Another little wail came from her crumpled face, and Melissa hugged her gently. 'Oh, darling, don't cry—are you hungry?'

The little head shook backwards and forwards.

'I am,' Melissa told her. 'I'm going to have some apple pudding.'

She snapped off the lid, dipped the spoon in and pretended to taste it. 'Mmm—lovely! Want some?'

Emily pursed her lips and turned away. Melissa repeated the performance, smacking her lips and making yum-yum noises, ignoring Emily, who was beginning to watch her. Finally a little hand reached up towards the spoon.

'Want some now? There's a little bit left—open wide—good girl!'

They 'shared' the rest of the jar, and when it was finished Emily cried for more. Melissa, however, was trapped because of the intravenous line. She leant forwards and called out of the door.

'Is there anybody there who can get me something?'

A large, unmistakably masculine shape filled

the doorway. 'Sure—what do you want?'

'Oh—hi. I was after another jar of baby food from the kitchen. I've got apple down her, but I think she needs some protein. If you ask one of the nurses they can find something.'

He nodded and disappeared, leaving her with the hungry, restless baby and a churning stomach. Damn him, he had no business being so attractive and so kind to her even when he was livid. . .

Seconds later he was back, a jar of chicken dinner in his hand. 'This do?'

'Wonderful—thanks.'

He handed her the opened jar and watched, propped against the wall, as she coaxed and cajoled and sang and played games—anything to get the food into the little scrap. Finally, with only a spoonful left, Melissa admitted defeat. 'Are we still doing fluid balance on her?' she asked Josh.

'No, not now. She's obviously stable. In fact the drip can probably come down, which will give her more freedom, and if her chest's OK today she can have the oxygen tent off. How do the burns look?'

'Pass. I haven't been here long. I'll get some fluids into her and then call you—we can check the dressings together, if you like. She'll be due for the cream at ten.'

'OK. If she looks good we'll take the drip down then.'

He went, and she wondered why she had been so worried about seeing him again today. The man who had hurled abuse at her last night seemed to have disappeared. Was he gone forever?'

Somehow she doubted it.

Emily took her drink well, and after she had settled her Melissa went to check on the pre-ops before finding Josh.

'Ready to do Emily now?' he asked, and she nodded.

'Do you have time?'

He laughed. 'Just about. Andrew Barrett wants me to go and have coffee with him in a while down in Outpatients, and I've got a million children to see between now and then, but I'm sure I can fit one more in. I'll come in in a tick.'

The dressings trolley was ready, and after washing her hands Melissa put gloves, gown and mask on and then very carefully and slowly removed the dressings. They hadn't really stuck, but the damaged skin was so tender that Emily cried pitifully, pulling her hands away, but Melissa persevered and gradually the dressings were removed.

The burns looked red and angry, with some fresh, oozing blisters over the backs of her hands and forearms, but the circulation to her fingers was good and the oedema in the tissues was only very slight.

Josh appeared and checked them, nodding. 'Looks good—she was a lucky girl. I think we'll take the drip out and give her oral paracetamol syrup for pain now. Just keep an eye on her fluids. Oh, by the way, her mother's not looking too good. They're talking of transferring her to Cambridge.'

'Oh, dear. Chest?' Melissa asked, smoothing ointment over Emily's arms.

He nodded, removing the strapping from the intravenous-drip site. 'And the burns—she's got third degree to fifteen per cent of her body, and second to a good bit more. She'll need massive grafting to cover it, if she makes it. She's got signs of toxaemia, too. I'm just going to pull the cannula out—good girl. Yes, it looks pretty grim for Mum, really.'

Melissa soothed Emily as Josh put a plaster over the little hole in her leg and kept pressure on it for a moment. 'You're telling me it's grim,' she murmured.

'It goes from bad to worse—do they think she'll make it?'

Josh shrugged. 'The physician in charge of her—Marumba, is it?—doesn't sound so hopeful today, according to the ITU sister. We'll just have to wait and see. In the meantime little Emily is going to need all the support we can give her.'

'Hmm. Well, as you said yourself, it's a case of having to make time, but I'm sure we can manage.' She secured the new dressings, scooped the little girl up and gave her a cuddle and a kiss. 'You're a good girl, aren't you?'

Emily buried her head in the angle of Melissa's neck, and Melissa felt a wave of love and compassion. 'Poor little scrap,' she murmured.

'At least she's got two parents,' Josh said quietly but pointedly.

So, he hadn't given up all conversation on the subject of their baby, she thought with a sigh, simply put it on hold in order to do his job. Well, what else had she really expected?

'Our baby will have two parents,' she said just as pointedly, and walked away from him, the little girl cradled in her arms. She put Emily back in her cot, settled her with the dummy her father had said she was used to and turned back to the door.

Josh was watching her, blocking her exit, clearly searching for words.

'You shouldn't be here. You've got to go to coffee with Andrew after you've seen a million children,' she reminded him a little stiffly.

'Yes, I know.' He searched her face with his midnight-blue eyes. 'About tonight. . .'

Her heart sank. 'What about tonight?'

'Are you in? We do have to talk.'

She felt a wave of panic wash over her. Could she

stand another session of being torn to pieces by him?
'I suppose we do,' she said reluctantly.

'I'll come round at seven, if that's all right, and I'll
bring a takeaway. What do you fancy?'

She shrugged. It was academic; she wouldn't have
any appetite, not with that conversation looming.
'Chinese?' she suggested.

'Done. I'll see you later.'

And he was gone, leaving her with a racing heart,
damp palms and a chronic case of heartburn.

CHAPTER THREE

JOSH was on time, and bearing not only a bag with the Chinese takeaway, but also a huge bunch of flowers.

He managed to negotiate the path this time without getting tangled up in the trees or tripping over the cat, and when Melissa opened the door he handed her the flowers, the half-smile on his lips at odds with the regret in his eyes.

'Just to say I'm sorry about last night,' he told her in a soft, raspy voice that for some inexplicable reason made her want to cry.

'Hey, chin up,' he said with an encouraging grin, and she blinked hard and sniffed and found a wobbly smile.

'They're lovely,' she told him, her voice choked. 'Thank you.'

'I would have brought them anyway—I'm just sorry my behaviour last night warranted an apology.'

She shrugged and turned away. 'You had every right to get angry. Under the circumstances I would have felt exactly the same.'

He followed her into the kitchen and the tiny room suddenly seemed even smaller. He set the carrier bag down on the worktop.

'Here—I didn't know what you would fancy, so I got all sorts of things.'

She stared at the bulging bag, and a bubble of laughter rose unexpectedly in her throat. 'I hope you're hungry, Josh.'

'Starving—but I always am. Anyway, you can put the left-overs in the fridge or feed them to Calico.'

'Him!' she said with a chuckle. 'Only if it's raw

steak or fresh rabbit—preferably on the hoof. He's disgustingly picky. The only thing he'll eat with any relish is cake.'

Josh shook his head. 'No cake. Oh, well, I'll have to struggle through it on my own. What a pity. Plates?'

She had some warming in the oven, and she had even dug out an old warming tray with nightlights under it when she had laid the table. He produced a bottle of wine—low alcohol, he said, so they could both drink it—and he opened the containers while she lit the nightlights and put the cover back on the warming tray.

'Pity it's still daylight—we could have had candles,' Josh said with a grin, and Melissa came back to earth with a bump.

What was she thinking about, setting the scene for a romantic dinner *à deux* with the man? He poured the wine and lifted his glass, but she refused to join in.

One eyebrow quirked. 'Not drinking?' he said softly.

'That depends on who or what you're drinking to.'

'How about us?'

Their eyes were locked, his mesmerising, hers trapped but determined.

'There is no us,' she told him, dragging her eyes away at last.

'But there could be.'

'No! Please, Josh, what's between us is over——'

'You're wrong, Lissa. It's hardly even started.'

She clutched her glass, wishing it were neat brandy instead of low-alcohol wine. 'It's over, Josh. The baby's a separate issue.'

'I don't think so,' he said, his voice very quiet. 'You and the baby are very much a part of the same issue for several years to come. And as I fully intend to be very much in evidence during my child's formative years, there's no way you can avoid me. That being the case, we need to work out a relationship we can both tolerate. I agree it's far too soon to talk about marriage, but I don't think we should exclude the possibility in the future——'

She set the glass down, pushed back her chair and stood up, all guns blazing. 'You aren't listening to me, are you? I am *not* looking for a husband. I don't *want* a husband, either now or in the future. I won't deny my child a father, for either of your sakes, but that's as far as it goes, Josh! That's as far as it will ever go!'

He twirled his glass for a moment, then looked up into her blazing eyes, his own face expressionless.

'Why don't you sit down and eat your supper before it's cold?' he said mildly, and took the wind completely out of her sails.

She gathered her faculties. 'I mean it, Josh.'

'I don't doubt you do. Anyway, I haven't offered to marry you yet, and with a temper like that maybe I won't. Come on, eat up, you're getting skinny as well as bad-tempered.'

'Skinny! I'm huge!'

He eyed her patiently. 'No, you're pregnant. You aren't huge by any stretch of the imagination. Now sit down and eat, please, so I can get stuck in, because I'm ravenous. I haven't eaten properly for forty-eight hours and I don't suppose you have either.'

Deprived of a co-operative adversary, she gave up her fight, subsided on to the chair and put a small spoonful of fried rice and a dollop of something with chicken, beansprouts and mushrooms on to her plate.

He sighed, clicked his tongue at her and put two king prawns in golden batter, a dribble of sweet and sour sauce and a handful of prawn crackers on the plate as well.

'That'll do for starters. Now eat, for God's sake.'

She did, suddenly starving, and loaded her plate

again twice before finally grinding to a halt.

'I told you you were hungry,' he said placidly, scooping up the last of the rice with a prawn cracker.

'I shall probably be sick.'

'Rubbish.'

He stood up, directed her to go and sit down, and cleared the table. She could hear him washing up and boiling the kettle, but she felt too well-fed and self-satisfied to bother to intervene. If he wanted to wait on her, let him. At least while he was in the kitchen, she wasn't having to answer awkward questions!

She was curled up on the chair with Calico on her lap when he came back in, set a mug down beside her and stretched out on the settee. 'I have eaten far too much,' he said emphatically, and, dropping his head back against the wing, he closed his eyes and sighed. 'I made tea,' he murmured. 'I thought you might still be off coffee.'

'I am—thanks.'

After a few minutes of companionable silence that she didn't dare take for granted, he opened his eyes, swallowed the last of his tea and set the mug down.

Here we go, she thought, the 'What are we going to do about custody?' question.

'Tell me about yourself,' he said instead, catching her completely by surprise.

'Me?'

He looked round the room in mock astonishment. 'Is there someone else here? Apart from me, who I know about, and the cat who, charming though he might be, rather pales into insignificance compared to my other priorities at the moment? Of course, you.'

'Why?' she asked suspiciously. 'Because you want ammunition in your court battle? You already know I've got the morals of an alley-cat after seducing you

on our second date—six times, as you were good
enough to point out. Why should I give you anything
else to hold against me?'

He chuckled. 'There's only one thing I'd like to
hold against you at the moment, and that's myself.
However, I get the feeling you'd be less encouraging
this time.'

She blushed and looked away.

'Stick to the subject,' she pleaded.

'Willingly. It wasn't me who changed it.'

'I'm very boring,' she warned him.

He smiled wryly. 'Let me be the judge of that. Come
on. Spill the beans.'

She sighed. He wasn't going to give up. She started
at the beginning, with her birth in London thirty-
four years before, her upbringing in Hampshire, her
boarding-school, her hobbies as a child, her teenage
hopes and aspirations, and before long she found herself telling him all about the loss of her parents in a
terrorist bombing while holidaying in the Middle East,
her disastrous marriage, the misery of her illness and
her desperation at learning she was unlikely ever to
bear a child.

'It's always been there, ever since I was tiny, the
knowledge that one day I would have children of my
own, and a husband and family—I suppose I thought
it was possible because my own parents were so happy
together.' She gave a bitter little laugh. 'Well, my husband blew away all my illusions of the ideal nuclear
family, but I still had this desperate, almost biological
need to be a mother.'

She looked up at him, trapped by his beautiful blue
eyes. 'Can you understand that?' She sighed and stared
blindly down at her hands, absently stroking the cat
on her lap. 'No, I don't suppose you can. Men feel
differently, don't they? With them it's more a need

to prove their masculinity, to show the world they're real men.'

She couldn't keep the bitterness out of her voice. God knows she had plenty to be bitter about. Her husband had left her because she wasn't what he called a real woman—she was no good in bed, she was always in pain and so was quiet and withdrawn instead of ready to party, and there was the constant threat to his masculinity if she should fail to conceive. Not that they had ever tried. Their marriage had been too fragile for her to dare risk a child's happiness and emotional security—and she wouldn't do so now.

'Your husband was a pretty lousy role model really, wasn't he,' Josh said quietly. It wasn't a question, but she answered it anyway.

'Perhaps he just had the courage to be honest about his feelings.'

Josh snorted. 'You think so? I don't; I think he was a coward. I think he was superficial, self-interested and an absolute bastard if you want the truth. Where was the compassion and support for you through your illness? Where was the understanding of the threat of infertility? And I bet you had intercourse whenever he demanded it, no matter how painful it was, just to prove that you could be a real wife.'

She blushed but said nothing. What could she say? As far as it went, he was absolutely right—and he was furious. Was that on her behalf? She was touched, but she had to set him straight.

'It wasn't really his fault,' she excused. 'He didn't get a very good bargain——'

'Bargain?' Josh yelled. 'For God's sake, Lissa—you were supposed to be partners, not part of a deal!'

She was astonished. 'Why are you so angry?' she asked him. 'He didn't do anything to you——'

'Didn't he?' he said, his voice soft now. 'If that's the case, why are you so set against marriage?'

She couldn't answer. A huge lump was sitting in her throat and blocking her words.

'Shall I tell you?' he went on, still softly. 'He poisoned you—intimidated and terrified you, dominated you, brutalised you and invalidated your worth as a woman. I'm beginning to see why you did what you did—and realise how much courage it took to come to me that weekend.'

He paused, then gave a ragged sigh. 'You asked if I could understand how you felt about having a child. Perhaps I'm more fortunate than you in that my faith in the opposite sex hasn't been destroyed by careless handling, so I still think there's a lot to be said for the nuclear ideal, the two-point-four kids and the wife and the dog and the roses round the door. It's nothing to do with proving my masculinity, it's about sharing, and not being lonely any more, having someone who cares if I come home at night. I suppose I'd always hoped that one day that special woman would come along. . .'

He trailed off, his voice wistful, and Melissa had the sudden devastating realisation of what she had done to him by taking the decision to become a parent away from him. It was all very well for her to vet him, but what chance had she given him? Perhaps a woman in indifferent health with a possibly inherited gynaecological disorder wasn't the mother he would have chosen for his child. And certainly this bizarre arrangement of single parenting didn't feature in his plans.

Guilt swamped her, and her eyes filled again. 'Oh, Josh, I've wrecked it for you, haven't I?' she whispered. 'Taken your dream and smashed it—I'm so sorry. . .'

His face blurred, and she bent her head and closed her eyes. She felt too tired and battered to cry again, too emotionally raw to deal with his pain as well as her own.

Then she felt his arms round her, cradling her against his chest.

'Lissa, hush,' he murmured. 'You haven't smashed anything.'

'I have—I've ruined your life, and I had no right——'

The cat, trapped between them, squawked indignantly and wriggled off her lap. Josh eased away to give him room, then lifted her and carried her to the settee, sitting down again with her on his lap, her head cradled firmly against his shoulder by the gentle pressure of one large, warm hand that cupped her nape and smoothed the hair soothingly. A hiccuping sob rose in her throat, and his arms tightened fractionally.

'Silly girl,' he murmured. 'You've got to stop crying or you're going to shrink with all this water.'

His kindness only made it worse, drenching her in remorse. She took a shuddering breath and dragged a hand through the straggling wilderness of her hair.

'Oh, God, I've been such a fool! If I could only turn the clock back——' Her voice cracked and his arms tightened again, rocking her against the broad expanse of his chest in a timeless gesture of comfort.

'Shhh. Lissa, hush, love, it's all right——'

'But it isn't!' she wailed. 'I've ruined your life!'

He gave a rueful chuckle. 'Hardly. You're going to have my baby—that might be an unexpected change of direction, but it's hardly going to ruin it. Anyway, as you so rightly pointed out, if I was that worried about it I could have made damn sure it didn't happen, and I didn't.'

She sniffed. 'I hardly gave you a chance.'

'Rubbish. I'd hate you to think you seduced me against my will and better judgement. I've got perfectly adequate brakes, sweetheart, I just didn't want to use them. In case you didn't notice, I was with you all the way, Lissa.'

She had noticed. She straightened up, levering herself away from his all too comfortable chest and wiping the tears from her cheeks with the backs of her hands. He handed her a tissue and she blew her nose and made herself meet his eyes.

They were gentle, almost loving, and she felt a heel.

'If only there was some way I could change it. . .'

'There is. You could give us a chance.'

Oh, lord, he meant it. She could tell by the sincerity of his voice and the emotion clearly written in his eyes.

'Josh, I can't——'

'You could. I'm not like your husband. I wouldn't hurt you, I promise. All I'm asking is an opportunity to find out if there's anything between us to build on.'

'No——'

'Please, Lissa, just hear me out. That weekend was something quite different to anything I'd ever experienced before. We just seemed to have something— something special, different. It would be such a shame to throw it all away without giving us a chance.'

She couldn't look at him. He wasn't begging, just quietly telling her from the heart how he felt about them, and it tore her to pieces because she had nothing to give him that was worth having. In the end, like her husband, he would be disillusioned, short-changed, and then he would leave her.

And this time the pain would be more than she could bear.

She stood up—she couldn't think while she was so close to him—and went over to the window. The sun was just dipping down below the horizon, and the sky was a blaze of colour.

Strange, when her world was all so grey.

'Josh, I can't,' she told him. 'Please don't ask me again.' Her voice was strangely calm now, quietly determined. Funny, that it could sound so confident when she was falling apart inside. 'There's nothing special between us; I was just acting. You've said yourself you could understand how desperate I was. I'm sorry if I've hurt you, but I really don't want a relationship.'

He was silent for so long that she thought he must have gone, but then she heard the creak of the settee, and his quiet footsteps going to the door.

'Just think about it,' he said. 'Don't close your mind to us in a reflex action. I know your husband hurt you, but I'm damned if I can see how he's earned the right to go on doing it.'

She heard the door open and close with a quiet click, then watched as he crossed the lawn, ducking under the apple tree and getting into his car. He reversed off the drive, turned in the lane and drove away into the sunset.

Just like the end of a weepy film, she thought, and then the colours in the sky blurred and ran together. . .

They were busy at work in the next couple of days. The routine cases decided to be less than routine, and the tricky ones got trickier.

Little Emily's mother was transferred to Cambridge and was desperately ill, and her father was torn between them both and needed a great deal of emotional support. So did Emily, who was healing well and settled happily in the ward but still cried for her mother whenever things got on top of her, which was quite often. She couldn't understand why her mother wasn't there, and there was no way to explain it to such a young child. Melissa found herself filling the gap, even to the point of carrying Emily round with her while she attended to some of the other children.

Fortunately she didn't have the toddler with her when one of the children in for tonsillectomy gave them a scare by haemorrhaging on the second day post-op, just before he was due to go home. He wouldn't eat, and Melissa was trying to coax him to have his lunch so he would be ready when his mother came.

The tonsillectomy children often refused food post-op because of their sore throats, but this little chap looked pale and Melissa was concerned about him. She noticed him swallowing frequently and he complained of feeling sick and having a nasty taste in his mouth, so she let him leave the table in the middle of the ward and climb back into his bed. She had a funny feeling about him, and just as she was about to look in his throat he was sick and confirmed her fears that he was haemorrhaging.

She jabbed the bell, laid him on his side so he could breathe and called for help, just as his poor mother arrived on the ward.

'Oh, my God! David! What's happened?' she practically screamed, rushing to the little boy's side.

Melissa looked up and gave her a reassuring smile. 'He'll be all right. It looks much worse than it is, really, but I'm afraid he'll have to go back to Theatre and have his throat resutured. Could you just keep his face turned down so he doesn't choke and stop him panicking while I contact the surgeon?'

She left the mother, sent Anna, her staff nurse, to look after them both and rang the ENT surgeon.

Within minutes little David was rushed up to Theatre for resuturing and had to have a blood transfusion just to be on the safe side.

He was returned to them mid-afternoon, wan but

very much alive, and his mother hardly dared to leave his side.

The repercussions among the other post-op tonsillectomy children and their parents were predictable but wearing, and Melissa found herself repeating the same reassuring conversation over and over again.

By contrast Josh gave her no trouble at all. He was there when necessary, quietly efficient, endlessly reliable and a thoroughly decent human being.

She felt dreadful.

She was also losing weight, as he had said. It was partly because they were so busy, but also because she didn't seem to get to the shops as regularly as she should, and so she often had nothing to eat at night except toast. She still hadn't been to the shops and it was nearly the end of the week. Maybe at the weekend. . .

On Friday afternoon, the end of his first week at the hospital, Josh found her slumped in her office, eyes closed, grabbing a few minutes' peace before tackling the supermarket.

'Lissa? Are you OK?' he asked urgently.

She opened her eyes and sighed. 'Yes—tired. I've got to go shopping, and I just can't be bothered.'

'Why don't you grab something in the canteen to save you having to cook tonight?' he asked.

She laughed. 'It's too far to walk. I haven't got that much energy.'

He frowned at her. 'You look awful,' he scolded. 'Go home now. I'll bring you something to eat.'

'No——'

'Yes. You're pregnant, with my baby. I have a vested interest in making sure you both stay well. Now scoot. I'll see you in an hour or so.'

She sighed again. Why was she disappointed because

he was only looking after the baby? She didn't want
him, for God's sake!

'Are you sure?' she asked.

'I never say anything I don't mean,' he told her, and
somehow she just knew it was true.

She dredged up a smile. 'Thanks, Josh. I'll see
you later.'

She dragged herself home, changed into a sloppy
old tracksuit and curled up on the sofa with Calico.
The next thing she knew there were noises in the
kitchen and Calico had gone off to investigate, tail
held straight up as he trotted through the door with a
welcoming squawk.

'He should have been a parrot,' she muttered, and,
struggling with the pins and needles in her feet, she
limped after the cat.

'Stone me,' she breathed, staring round the kitchen.
'Who are you feeding, an army?'

'No—just one stupid woman and a heavily depen-
dent child,' he retorted.

There were shopping bags on every surface, and he
was squatting in front of the open fridge, lobbing stale
cheese and mouldy bread into the bin. 'My God,
woman, it's a miracle you haven't got cholera.'

'I don't think you get cholera from not eating,' she
said drily. 'Josh, just what are you doing?'

'Making sure you have an adequate diet. Pass me
that bag—on second thoughts, don't; it's heavy.' He
stood up, grabbed two bags and unloaded them swiftly
into the fridge.

Yoghurts, cheeses, low-fat spread, milk, salad
ingredients, cold meats, fresh steak—steak?

'Don't let Calico see that,' she advised. 'He'll get it
out of the fridge and eat it.'

'Only if he's quick—I'm cooking it in five minutes.'

He continued to shovel food into the fridge, then

stood up, unpacked several tins and jars and hunted for an obvious spot.

'In here,' she said, opening a door at the end and showing him an empty larder.

'My God—what were you going to eat tonight?' He hefted a rather tired-looking can of sardines and another of cat food, and scowled at her. 'Melissa, you have to take this more seriously.'

She shrugged helplessly. 'I do mean to. I've just been so busy, and by the time we finish at the end of the day I'm so tired——'

'Maybe you should give up work, or cut your hours.'

She shook her head. 'I don't want to.'

'Do you want to lose the baby?'

Her eyes widened with shock. 'Of course not——'

'Then you've got to be sensible. We'll start with your appalling diet. Here, stack this lot where you want them while I put the rest away. Where's your freezer?'

'I haven't got one—only the top of the fridge.'

He sighed. 'Lissa, I despair. What about your neighbours?'

She looked at him in blank astonishment. 'What about them?'

'Never mind.' He grabbed two bags, marched out of the kitchen and up the path, then disappeared round the end of the hedge. A few minutes later he was back, empty-handed.

'They'll store the stuff for you until your freezer arrives.'

'What freezer?'

He glared at her. 'The one I'm about to order— and don't you dare argue!'

He pushed past her into the sitting-room, thumbed through her phone-book and picked up the phone. Moments later he came back.

'It'll be delivered tomorrow—only a small one that

will fit easily in the larder if I take out those two bottom shelves. . .they're empty anyway, so you can hardly object.' He went into the larder and started tugging at the shelves.

She folded her arms over her chest and glared at his back. 'Would it make any difference if I did?'

'Probably not. Have you got a screwdriver?'

'Not handy, or I'd probably have stabbed you with it.'

He straightened up, bumping his head on a shelf, and swore under his breath. 'Are you by any chance mad at me?' he said mildly.

She skipped the obvious answer to that, heading straight for the reason. 'You're interfering,' she said.

'I have——'

'I know, a vested interest.' She turned away, clearing the dishes into the dishwasher. He had bought new powder, so she could put it on at last instead of using it as a store for dirty crocks until she had the energy to deal with them. She slammed it shut, twisted the knob and listened with satisfaction as it began doing her least favourite job.

He was swirling oil in a pan when she turned round.

'What are you doing?' she asked, as if it wasn't perfectly obvious.

'Cooking our supper.'

It sounded shockingly intimate. 'Is there anything you'd like me to do?' she found herself asking. Hell, why didn't she just throw him out? Apart from the fact that he'd just spent a fortune on all this food and so had more right to it than she did——

'You could make a salad.'

She swallowed. 'Right. Salad.'

She selected some ingredients, washed and dried them and tore them into chunks, chopping the cucumber and tomato and throwing them on top.

'Did you buy any dressing?'

He shook his head. 'I'll make it—go and clear the table.'

'Yes, sir.'

She could smell the steak that was sizzling in the pan, and the part-baked rolls crisping in the oven, and her mouth watered. Lord, she was starving! She had just scooped the paperwork off the table and found some cutlery when he appeared with the salad in one hand and crispy garlic rolls in the other.

'How do you like your steak?'

'Anyhow,' she said. 'I just like it.'

He reappeared with two plates and set one down in each place.

'It's a pity we haven't got any mustard,' she said thoughtfully.

He vanished, returning with a jar of whole-grain mustard in his hand. '*Voilà!*'

She smiled at him. 'You missed your vocation—you should have been a conjurer.'

He grinned. 'I do magic shows for the kids sometimes—Christmas, New Year, that sort of thing. It keeps them amused. Eat up.'

She did, stunned by how hungry she was and how wonderful it all tasted. 'I was ravenous,' she told him.

'Mmm—undernourished, like I said. Can you manage a yoghurt?'

'Mmm. Strawberry—or peach.'

'Picky, eh? Like the damn cat.'

There was no sign of the cat. 'Where is he?' Melissa asked his retreating back.

'In here, eating his bit of steak.'

'He's what?'

She shot to her feet and followed him through to the kitchen. Sure enough, Calico was crouched down, tucking into a few nice, juicy strips of raw steak.

'You spoilt cat,' she said indulgently.

Josh just grunted. 'I'm cultivating an ally,' he explained, and handed her a yoghurt. 'Here, eat this while I take these shelves out before I forget.'

He went out to his car and came back a few moments later with a screwdriver with which he proceeded to demolish her larder.

'There,' he said, standing back and admiring his handiwork. 'Just the job. Where shall I stick the shelves?'

She raised one eyebrow, and he chuckled. 'Keep it clean, Lissa. Do you have a shed?'

'Yes, thank you.'

He held out his hand. 'Key?'

'It's not locked. There's nothing much in it since the lawnmower was nicked.'

'I wonder why,' he said drily, and disappeared out of the back door.

She looked round the kitchen at the food still waiting to be put away, and sighed. It was very kind of him, and she knew why he was doing it, but she hated feeling beholden to him. After all, it was her decision, her pregnancy—her baby.

She laid a hand over the small curve of her abdomen. It wasn't really big enough yet to be called a bump, but it was definitely there. She wondered what it was, and whether it would ever forgive her for the apparently cold-blooded way she had gone about its conception.

'I love you. Please believe me, it was the only way,' she said quietly, staring down at where it lay under her hand.

It might have been because she was so focused on it at that moment, or simply coincidence, but in that instant she felt a very slight but quite distinct movement inside her. She lifted her head, like a doe scenting the breeze, totally focused on the sensation.

'God, that shed is a mess! I hate to think how many spiders live in it—— Lissa?' He grabbed her shoulders gently, staring down at her with worried eyes. 'Sweetheart, what's wrong?'

The panic in his voice cut through her absorption, and she met his eyes, a radiant smile lighting her face.

'It moved,' she whispered, awestruck. 'I felt the baby move.'

Something happened in his face, something incredible and wonderful and desperately revealing, and then he folded her into his arms and held her as if she was unbelievably precious.

'Is it the first time?' he said gruffly.

She nodded, and then because he couldn't see her she murmured, 'Yes—yes, it is. I can feel it again— it's so strong I can't believe I haven't noticed till now.'

Without thinking, without reservation or hesitation, she took his hand and laid it low down over the little curve. There was another movement, like the flutter of a bird's wing.

'There—did you feel it?'

She tipped her head back and looked up in time to see a rapt expression on his face.

'Oh, Lissa,' he murmured, and then something shifted in his eyes, and his hand slid round behind her and drew her up against him just as his head came down.

'Josh,' she murmured, but his lips cut off her protest, if that was what it had been meant to be, and then she was tasting him again, clinging to him and winding her fingers through his hair, holding him steady while she took all he offered and demanded more.

His tongue traced her teeth and she opened her mouth, drawing him in and suckling gently. He groaned, a low, ragged sound that was lost against her lips, and heat exploded in her body. With a little cry she arched against him, loving the feel of him hard against her soft curves, needing to be closer still, holding him, drawing him into her until they were one. . .

His lips left hers, moving over her face, leaving a trail of hot, languid kisses over the fevered skin of her throat. Hands, warm and dry and firm, slid up under her top and round, cupping her full, soft breasts as an untidy sigh was torn from his throat.

'You are so very, very beautiful,' he said raggedly, and then his mouth fastened over one swollen, aching peak and suckled gently.

She cried out, her knees buckling, and he caught her against his chest. Lifting his head, he looked down into her eyes, his own burning like blue flames, and traced her cheek with one trembling finger.

'Are we going to bed,' he asked softly, 'or are you about to remember that you just invented your response before?'

Common sense slowly seeped back into her like cold water. 'Oh, God,' she groaned, and, closing her eyes, she tipped her head forwards on his chest and let out a shaky sigh.

His arms cradled her gently, letting her come back down to earth in her own time, and when she felt she could stand again she eased away from him and he let her go.

She hugged her arms round herself, missing the comfort of his broad, solid chest. 'I'm sorry,' she whispered. 'I didn't mean to let that happen.'

'I didn't mean to do it, but I don't intend to flagellate myself over it, either. You're beautiful, Lissa—and you're pregnant with my child. You can't blame me for wanting you.'

'It mustn't happen again,' she said automatically. 'You mustn't come here again; it's not fair on either of us.'

'Someone has to look after you if you won't do it.'

'I will! I just haven't had time—by the way, what do I owe you for the shopping?'

He made a disgusted noise, and so she thanked him, rather stiffly.

'Stow it, Lissa,' he muttered. 'You know why I did it. Now I'm going before I do something I'll regret.'

He drove off into the sunset again, but this time she didn't want to cry, she wanted to scream and rant and rip the walls down, because what she really wanted to do was hold him in her arms and take him to bed and make love to him until the sun came up again—and it was the last thing in the world she could let herself do. . .

CHAPTER FOUR

'So, how's the freezer?'

Melissa looked up from the jigsaw she had been commandeered to help with and marvelled yet again at the colour of Josh's eyes.

'Very pretty,' she told him.

He stared at her for a second. 'Pretty?'

'Mmm. A definite asset to the larder.'

He shifted his gaze to the jigsaw, found the piece of sky she was looking for and neatly slotted it into place. 'Is it working?'

'I expect so,' she said. 'Or, at least, I expect it would, if I had anywhere to plug it in. Unfortunately I don't. Anyway, it doesn't matter, because it's very decorative. Now, how did you find that piece? We've been looking for it for ages.'

He grinned, straightened up and gave a cheeky shrug. 'I'm just naturally brilliant.'

'So how come,' she asked, standing up herself and meeting his eyes challengingly, 'you failed to notice that there wasn't a socket in the larder?'

'Ah.' He grinned again. 'Let's say I was distracted by much more interesting things.'

The warmth in his eyes did funny things to her insides. She looked away quickly.

'Talking of more interesting things, I think Emily looks ready to go home,' she told him, 'but the trouble is her mother's still in Cambridge, father's staying up there and I'm not sure we can discharge her to the relatives who have got her big brother. The woman seems a bit daffy, and she still needs sterile dressings on that left arm for a while.'

'So keep her in.'

She looked up at him in surprise. 'We have enormous pressure on beds.'

'I'll have a chat to Social Services. Maybe they can put her with a foster family for a little while, until her burns are completely healed and her mother's more stable.'

'But that means another change of carer. Poor little thing, she's just got used to all of us.'

He shrugged. 'So we'll keep her for a few more days. The bed state's not that drastic at the moment. If the worst comes to the worst, community nurses could go into her home and change the dressings. Where is she?'

Melissa smiled. 'In the garden. She's having a wonderful time out there on the slide with another little tot. One of the play assistants is with them. I expect she's exhausted!'

He smiled back, his eyes softening, and he was about to say something else when his bleep went off.

With a muttered apology he went over to the phone, called the switchboard and within seconds was leaving the ward.

'Asthmatic—better get a bed ready,' he called over his shoulder, and then he was gone.

'Hi-ho, hi-ho—as if we didn't have enough to do with the elective ops and the overnight crises!' Anna grumbled goodnaturedly.

There was a bed ready, but they didn't need it. Josh reappeared on the ward with a tight-lipped 'don't ask' expression on his face. Melissa said nothing, merely took him on the ward round and checked the patients for discharge, looked at those long-stay patients who were not yet able to go home and then went into the kitchen.

She closed the door behind them, made a pot of tea and waited. It didn't take long.

'He was twelve,' Josh began in a low, tight voice laced with impotent fury. 'He forgot to take his medicine last night, and didn't have his inhaler at school. The attack started during his first lesson—he was sitting next to someone who has a cat at home. The teacher didn't worry too much at first, but then he got worse, so they sent him to the secretary. She couldn't get his mother so she called the doctor, he called the ambulance, it got held up at some road works and bingo—the child arrived in status asthmaticus, and there was nothing we could do. Nothing. Not a single, solitary damn thing——'

He broke off, his jaw working furiously as he struggled against his anger and helplessness.

'I'm sorry,' Melissa said quietly.

Josh gave her a faint, weary smile. 'What a bloody start to the week. Oh, damn, damn, damn, damn, damn. . .' He stared sightlessly past her, his eyes emptied of everything except someone else's pain.

She didn't think or hesitate. She walked over to him, laid her head on his chest and hugged him. After a second his arms came round her, holding her closer, and he settled his head against hers.

She could feel his cheek against her forehead, the slight scrape of stubble as he moved his head a fraction. He was wearing aftershave, a light, elusive fragrance, slightly citrussy with a faint tang of musk that teased at her senses. His heart was slow and steady beneath her ear, and his arms felt good around her—strong and secure, and somehow absolutely right.

It scared her to bits. What was she doing, allowing herself to get this close to him? She was supposed to be keeping him at a distance, but how could she have ignored the plea in his eyes? She was about to move out of his arms when he spoke again, his voice a low, quiet rumble against her ear.

'It was worse this time than it's ever been,' he said slowly. 'I don't know if it's because you're having my baby, but this time it just seemed much sharper, somehow.' He let out a heavy sigh. 'The last time I lost a child I didn't know I was going to be a father. I wonder if that's got anything to do with it?'

He was thinking out loud, she realised, sounding out his feelings. She said nothing, just held him, and he carried on.

'Do you know, Lissa, I was stunned at how much difference it made—how much more it hurt? Just to be able to put myself in the parents' shoes more easily. . .' He gave a short, bitter laugh. 'I used to think I could empathise, but I didn't even come close before.'

She tightened her arms in a hug. 'I'm sure you did. You're a very warm person, a good communicator. I've seen you with parents. I'm sure your performance hasn't changed, except maybe from the inside. Now, perhaps, you just feel it more for them. I know I do.'

He lifted his head and looked down at her. 'So it's not just my imagination?'

She shook her head. 'No. No, I've felt a change, as well. Not to the children, but to the parents. I'm more tolerant of their anxieties, somehow.'

He grinned slowly. 'Their panic seems much more reasonable. Although this time——' He broke off, and the grin faded. 'Losing a child is always more than just a professional failure. Somehow with adults you can distance yourself, but with kids—hell, sometimes I think I'll never be able to do it easily.'

'I don't think you should. I don't think we ought to be able to give up on a life—any life—easily. On the other hand, we ought to know when to let go. That's hard, too—sometimes harder.'

He nodded. 'I've done some palliative care—I had to get out. It tore me to bits. It was get out or get hard, and I didn't want to do that.'

As if suddenly conscious that they were still standing with their arms round each other, he dropped a light kiss on her forehead and let her go.

Her arms felt desperately empty all of a sudden, and she busied herself with her cup.

'Don't forget your drink,' she reminded him.

He picked up his cup and drained it, then gave her a wry, weary wink. 'Thanks for the tea and sympathy.'

'My pleasure.'

The door opened and closed softly, and she was left alone in the little kitchen with nothing but her thoughts and the faint, elusive scent of his aftershave. . .

Melissa heard his car on the drive shortly before seven that evening, just as she was grappling with the exhausting notion of making herself a meal. Her heart sank. She would be obliged to offer him a meal as well, and she really couldn't be bothered to cook anything proper. . .

Dredging up a weary smile, she opened the door and stared at him. He had a roll of cable in one hand, a toolkit in the other, and a small posy of flowers in his teeth.

He mumbled something totally unintelligible.

She took the flowers out of his mouth. 'What?'

Josh grinned. 'I said, would you like to take the flowers? I've brought some stuff so I can put you a socket in the larder.'

She eyed the cable doubtfully. 'Shouldn't I get an electrician?'

He tutted. 'Oh, ye of little faith,' he grumbled. 'It'll

be fine.' He put the toolbox down on the kitchen floor, put the cable on top of it and studied the freezer in minute detail. 'Looks good, doesn't it?' he said with satisfaction. 'Just the right size.'

'Like I said, very pretty. I also gather it was paid for,' she said drily.

He grinned. 'I could hardly buy you a present and then expect you to pay for it, could I?'

There was no answer to that, so she put the kettle on, arranged the little posy of flowers and watched as he drilled and screwed and tapped and stripped wires and cut himself and swore softly——

'Cup of coffee?' she offered.

'How about neat whisky?' he growled, sucking the end of his thumb.

'I haven't got any.'

'The coffee would be lovely—— Ouch, damn.'

He banged his head on the shelf above him, wriggled out backwards and stood up.

'I knew I should have got an electrician,' she murmured provocatively.

His eyes narrowed. 'Don't push your luck,' he muttered menacingly, and almost snatched the coffee from her.

Somehow she wasn't in the least bit scared of him. 'I suppose,' she said, enjoying herself now and feeling much better, 'that you'd like some supper?'

The grumbling discontent on his face gave way to a boyish grin. 'Now, how did you guess?'

'Pork chops in cider and apple, with new potatoes and broccoli?'

His stomach gave a very satisfactory grumble, and she grinned. 'Fine. Let me get it under way in the oven, and you can finish off while it cooks—or will you need the power off?'

He shook his head. 'Not for long. I'm working back

towards the socket I'm taking a spur off. Five minutes, maybe? If that.'

The power was off for three minutes, the freezer worked straight away, there were no flashes and bangs and Melissa was frankly amazed. She said so as they sat down to eat their meal.

He rolled his eyes. 'You don't have any faith in me, do you? I was raised with good, solid practical skills on my parents' farm—talking of which, they'd like to meet you.'

Her eyes widened. 'Your parents?' she said in astonishment. 'What do they know about me?'

'Only what I've told them.'

She swallowed. 'Which is?'

'That we had an affair and you're pregnant.'

She closed her eyes. 'Great,' she mumbled.

'Well, there didn't seem to be any point in not telling them that. What am I supposed to do, turn up one day with the baby in tow and say I found it? For God's sake, Lissa, they're going to be grandparents.'

That was a complication that Melissa hadn't even considered. Being an only child and her own parents having died many years before, she had considered raising the baby in an atmosphere free of other relatives. Suddenly she realised that with Josh's involvement, the baby was going to have a whole family she had never met who would want to share in its upbringing—grandparents, uncles and aunts, cousins. . .the list was endless.

'How many?' she asked feebly.

'How many what?'

'Others—brothers, sisters, that sort of thing.'

'I've got two brothers and three sisters, all younger than me——'

'Six?' she shrieked. 'There are six of you?'

'Yes—and Mum lost two as well in the middle.

That's why there's a gap after the girls before my little brother Matthew—he's fifteen now. Michael's married to Ellie, as you know, Sarah's married to Chris and Lottie's married to Alastair, so that's eleven of us if you don't count the hairy nerd.'

'The what?'

He grinned. 'My youngest sister Hannah's at art college and living with a bloke that my parents don't approve of. God knows what his name is—he's known as the hairy nerd.'

She giggled despite her misgivings. 'Does he know that?'

'I don't suppose so,' Josh said drily. 'Hannah's too sensible to expose him to the family.'

'Any nephews and nieces?' she asked, dreading the answer.

'Mike and Ellie have got a baby due any day now— in fact it's a bit overdue, I think. I'm waiting to hear. And Sarah and Chris have got one of each. Al and Lottie are waiting until she's done her SHO.'

'Another doctor?'

'Uh-huh. Sarah's a nurse, her husband's a GP. Michael's a civil engineer, and Matthew wants to be a vet if he doesn't go into the farm with my father. They want him to, of course, but they won't stop him doing whatever he wants.' He stretched his arms wide in an expansive gesture. 'So, that's the Lancasters for you. Thirteen and a half of us, and the hairy nerd.'

Melissa swallowed. So many! She wondered rather blankly what it would be like to have such an enormous family—and getting bigger.

'At least this baby won't be their only grandchild,' she said cautiously.

'God no! I expect they'll end up with dozens. Why?'

Melissa shook her head. She couldn't explain the feeling of dread she had, the terror that her baby would be taken out of her control and absorbed into Josh's huge and complicated family, leaving her out in the cold. Would their warmth lure the baby, so that she wanted to be with them, not her? A terrible panic filled her, and she pushed her plate away and knotted her hands together in her lap.

Josh was beside her in seconds. 'Lissa?' he murmured. 'Sweetheart, what is it?'

'It's my baby,' she mouthed. 'My baby.'

He was silent for a second, then he sank down on to his haunches beside her and tilted her face round to meet his eyes. 'Nobody's going to take your baby away from you,' he said slowly and clearly. 'Nobody. But he will have a family— a family that will want to love him and share things with him. You can't deny him that.'

'Her,' she corrected automatically.

'Her, then. Do you mind if it's a boy?'

She made herself meet his eyes. 'Why? Do you have influence there, as well?'

He grinned slightly. 'Not much.' Then his expression clouded. 'What do you mean, as well?'

She looked away. 'I was talking to Andrew Barrett. I gather you've known him for years.'

'Yes. That was how I found you. I rang and asked if he knew a paediatric nurse called Melissa——'

She spun back towards him. 'And he told you? Just like that?'

'Yes—Lissa, it wasn't his fault! I made it sound like idle curiosity. I said I'd met you briefly in London at the beginning of the year.'

'So how come the job?'

He shrugged. 'It was available, I was already looking and he'd heard that. In fact he was about to ring me and ask if I was interested. I would have been interested even without knowing you worked here, so it's quite possible we would have ended up as colleagues anyway.'

'Your precious coincidence again.'

'That's right. Now, getting back to my parents, how about Saturday?'

'Where do they live?'

'Near Orford, on the coast. It won't take them long to get here.'

'Here?' she shrieked, her panic rising. 'Why here?'

He sighed, stood up and started clearing the table. 'Because it's only natural they should want to see where the baby's going to be brought up. I think they have a right to know that their grandchild is going to be properly cared for——'

'Properly—damn you, Joshua Lancaster, this is my baby! I never asked you to get involved, and I'm damned if I'm running around all day tarting the place up and scrubbing my fingers to the bone just to satisfy two people I've never even met that I'll be a proper mother!'

She glared at him, the silence ringing with her angry words, and he shook his head slowly. 'Did I ask you to? The place is fine——'

'It's a mess. I haven't got the energy to clean it the way it needs doing——'

'So get a cleaning lady.'

She stared at him. 'Josh, I can't afford a cleaning lady. I own the house, because it's what I was left from my parents after my divorce settlement. I know it's nothing fantastic, but it's warm and cosy and——'

'It's a lovely house. What do you mean, it's what you were left after your divorce settlement?'

She looked blankly at him. 'What?'

'Explain your divorce settlement.'

'Oh. That. I got half of everything.'

'Of your parents' house?'

'No. We'd already sold that because it was too far away to live in, and anyway he didn't like it. He wanted a trendy waterfront studio in London.'

'So you sold your family home, bought a flat and when he left you he generously gave you half back.'

She sighed. 'Yes.' She tried to keep the bitterness out of her voice, but talk of her divorce and how she had lost so much always upset her.

Apparently it upset Josh, too, if the tight line of his mouth was anything to go by.

She shrugged. 'I didn't make a very good wife——'

He smacked his hand down flat on the table, making her jump. 'Stop it!' he ordered furiously. 'Stop denigrating yourself and putting yourself down and thinking that you're worthless! Damn, if I could get just five minutes with that man——!'

He stalked into the kitchen, leaving her sitting at the table faintly stunned. She had hated selling her family home and she knew she had lost even more in the divorce, but she had never for a moment thought that her ex-husband wasn't entitled to it. Now, though, she began to wonder if he hadn't perhaps had his eye on her money all along, and had seen divorcing her and making off with half the goodies as a close second to marriage to a woman he discovered he couldn't love.

'Well, there's a thing,' she murmured to herself, and, gathering up the last few dishes, she went into the kitchen.

'Please don't wreck all my crockery,' she said mildly as Josh all but threw the plates into the dishwasher.

'Bloody man,' he growled.

'I think maybe I agree with you,' she said calmly, and took the plates out of his hand before he smashed them. 'However, it doesn't solve the problem of your parents. Can't we meet on neutral territory?'

'No. I'm sorry. It has to be here.'

She tried, but she couldn't shift him. In the end they compromised. He would clean the house, cook the meal and clear up, and she would arrange the flowers, put on a pretty dress and look decorative.

It seemed a reasonable trade.

It was actually a surprisingly easy evening. Melissa felt much of the heat was taken off her because Michael's wife, Ellie, had produced a little girl two days previously and it was almost all Josh's parents could talk about.

They were wonderful. Warm, funny, undemanding, they took her under their wing without criticism or condemnation, and by the time they left she was feeling truly wretched about her part in depriving them of a normal wife for their son and mother for their grandchild.

She was also very conscious of the fact that Josh had told them a severely limited edition of the truth.

After they went, she challenged him.

He laughed a little bitterly. 'What was I supposed to say? "Oh, by the way, we didn't know each other when we fell into bed, but she just decided she wanted a baby so she thought I'd do." I don't think they're quite that liberal-minded.'

She lifted her shoulders in a helpless shrug. 'I just felt bad for deceiving them. They're so nice.'

'They are nice—they're genuinely good, decent, loving people, and if you do anything at all to destroy their happiness, like denying them access to their grandchild, I'll——'

He broke off, clamping his jaw on the angry words, but Melissa wanted to hear them anyway, so she goaded him.

'You'll what? Take me to court? Go on, Josh, say

it! Get it out of your system. Stop being so damn nice to me all the time!'

'Why should I?' he asked deceptively quietly. 'Because you'd feel better then? Would it assuage your guilt, is that it?'

'Yes, damn it! Yes!'

He stared at her, her words ringing in the quiet cottage, and after a moment she sank down on to the chair and buried her face in her hands.

'Go home, Josh, please? I could do with some peace and quiet.'

He didn't. Instead he went into the kitchen without another word and finished the clearing up, then came back and set a cup of tea down beside her.

'Thank you for letting them come here and meet you,' he said quietly. 'It was very important for them to get to know you and to see the house. If it helps, they think you're a lovely girl, and a very welcome addition to the family.'

'But I'm not in the family,' she argued tiredly.

'But you could be.' He dropped on to his haunches in front of her and took one hand, absently caressing the back of it with his thumb. 'I know it hasn't been very long, but I love you, Lissa, and I want you to marry me.'

She stared at him in horror for a moment, then snatched her hand back. 'No! Josh, I told you——'

'Shh. Lissa, calm down. Just think about it.'

'No!'

He gave a heavy sigh and straightened up. 'I'll see you on Monday. In the meantime, just consider all the benefits of being part of a family, both for you and for the baby.'

The door shut behind him with a deafening little click, and she was suddenly completely alone.

*   *   *

Damn. He hadn't meant to push her. As soon as he'd said the words he knew it was a mistake. Her eyes had widened with panic and she had pulled back from him, not just physically but emotionally, reeling herself back in and retreating into her shell again—not that she ever came very far out, but she was beginning to trust him a little more and now he'd blown it.

Damn and blast.

He drove down to London, banged on his brother's front door and spent the rest of the night cramped on a sofa, his feet dangling in free space, wondering what the hell he was going to do while Michael, the cause of all his problems, snored peacefully in the next room surrounded by a welter of baby equipment and instant photos of a tiny little girl with a boot-button nose and startlingly blue eyes.

CHAPTER FIVE

THE next few weeks were very fraught for Melissa. She was finding work more and more tiring, and Josh's proximity was very much a two-edged sword. He was an excellent colleague, thoughtful, considerate and with a wonderful sense of humour that intervened just when things were getting too much for her.

He never failed to make her smile, however hard she tried to fight it, and that made her feel even guiltier.

He didn't say any more about marrying her, but she knew the subject was far from closed, and every now and again his mother would ring and ask how things were going, just to turn the knife.

On the work front, apart from being so tired she found she was enjoying the job and giving it more than ever, perhaps because motherhood was now so much closer to home.

Little Emily, the toddler with burns, went to a foster family with her older brother, because the relative he had been with was unable to look after them both for long. Melissa was delighted, because the foster mother was one she had met before in the course of her work and she was a thoroughly sensible, very loving person and Emily took to her instantly.

As she watched Josh at work with the children and their worried parents her admiration for him increased enormously.

He was a truly gifted, natural paediatrician, not only wonderful at calming terrified and pain-racked children but also an intuitive diagnostician. He just seemed to know almost instinctively when the illness was really serious, and when it wasn't, even though it might appear to be.

This was demonstrated very ably at the beginning of September, a month after he had joined the team

A boy of ten had been admitted for investigations, and as they were walking away from him after chatting briefly to his mother Josh turned and glanced back over his shoulder at the child, then looked at Melissa, his eyes troubled.

'His mother's worried. I think she feels he's got something really nasty.'

'Toby? He's had tonsillitis almost continuously this year,' Melissa told him. 'They can't seem to clear the infection up for any length of time at all, but some kids are like that. I expect she's just worrying about him needing an operation.'

He shook his head. 'No, I think it's more than that. Do you know his previous history?'

'Didn't the mother say he'd first had it when he was four?'

'Mmm. But since?' Josh's face grew thoughtful. 'Come into your office. I just want to look something up.'

He took down a copy of Nelson's *Paediatrics* from the shelf, thumbed through it and read quietly for a while, then sighed. 'Well, I hope I'm right.'

'What?'

He met her eyes, his own troubled. 'I think he's got chronic infectious mononucleosis, but, if I'm wrong, it could be leukaemia. One thing's for sure, he's got more than tonsillitis.'

A cold chill ran over her. 'Josh, surely it couldn't be leukaemia?'

'Why not?'

She shook her head. 'No reason. Oh, dear. Still, it

might be glandular fever, I suppose, but wouldn't the GP have picked glandular fever up?'

He shrugged. 'Depends what the mother said to him, how well he knows the child, if he thought it was just another kid with recurrent tonsillitis or if the symptoms weren't there to pick up. Has he been tested for glandular fever? If so, was the test negative? The mother's worried, though. She seemed really glad something was going to be done, as if she thought it was serious.' He stood up and shut the book. 'I'm going to have another chat to them—perhaps I'll clerk him if Rob hasn't got that far yet?'

Melissa shook her head. The houseman was still fairly inexperienced and took a long time to make his way round the new admissions.

Thus armed with an excuse, Josh disappeared, notes in hand, and found her a little while later in the treatment-room, changing a dressing.

'Could I have a word?' he said quietly.

'Anna, could you take over, please?' she asked, and, stripping off her gloves, she went with him to her office.

'Well?'

'He's got glands up all over the place. He's definitely got grotty tonsils, but I don't think they're what's making him ill at the moment, I think they're just a symptom.'

'So what do you think?'

He pursed his lips thoughtfully. 'Chronic glandular fever looks likely, except he's outside the normal age range and he's certainly quite seriously ill. He's also, more worryingly, got a palpable, tender spleen and enlarged liver, and some unexplained bruising, although a boy of ten is quite likely to be smothered in bruises anyway, except these are quite new. The thing is, he hasn't been running around engaging in normal activities recently, so the bruises are possibly symptomatic.'

'But not of glandular fever.'

'No. We'll have to do bloods, but I do hope to God he hasn't got acute lymphoblastic leukaemia, because if he has, from the state he's in, frankly, I'd say the prognosis is lousy. On the other hand, if it's glandular fever he's still ill but he'll definitely get over it provided he doesn't rupture that spleen. It's very large—worryingly so. I'll have a word with Andrew about where we go from here.'

Andrew Barrett arrived on the ward within minutes, listened to what Josh had to say and then contacted the ENT surgeon and a haematologist. They held a case conference, and agreed on a whole battery of blood tests.

Melissa and Josh were just leaving the treatment-room after catheterising a little boy when the mother approached him.

'It isn't tonsillitis, is it?' she said. 'It's something much worse. I know it is. I've known for weeks.'

'What makes you say that?' Josh asked her gently.

'He's just not himself. It's not just an infection. He's been ill before; I know about infections. This is different,' she insisted. 'He's—sicker, somehow. As if he's fading away—leaving us. Especially since yesterday. He's going downhill so fast—he looks so pale now, waxy. . . I've just got a terrible, sinking feeling he's going to die, and nobody will listen to me.'

She looked up at them, her eyes pleading. 'What's wrong with my son? Why won't any of you tell me the truth?'

'Because we don't know for sure—not yet,' Josh told her. 'It may just be tonsillitis, or it may be compounded by a persistent form of glandular fever.'

'Or it might be leukaemia,' the mother said flatly.

Josh and Melissa exchanged glances. 'I don't think it's likely,' he murmured.

'But it's possible.'

Josh hesitated, then nodded. 'Yes, maybe it's possible.'

His voice was gentle, but the colour drained from her face.

'Oh, God. Well, thank you for not lying to me.'

'It probably isn't,' Josh explained. 'I really don't think it is, but you're right, he is very ill.'

'I know.' She laughed, a strained, tragic little sound. 'I'll try not to worry. That's what you all say, isn't it? "Don't worry, it may not be anything serious." Roughly translated, it means, "Gird your loins, we'll tell you the whole truth when we've had time to work out what to say." I suppose you're now going to offer me a cup of tea—that's the usual form, isn't it? A cup of tea and a box of strategically placed tissues——'

The tears started to trickle down her face, and, putting his arm round her shoulder, Josh guided her into the office and pushed her gently down on to a chair. Melissa closed the door, sat down beside Toby's mother and put her arm round her heaving shoulders.

After a while she sat up straight, sniffed and took the proferred tissues from the strategically placed box. With a wan smile, she thanked them and then systematically shredded the tissue in her lap.

'Is that your first baby?' she said to Melissa.

Melissa's hand automatically slipped round and cradled her child protectively. 'Yes—yes, it is.'

'Just imagine how you would feel if your baby was sick, and nobody would tell you the truth. How would you and your husband feel?'

Melissa exchanged an anguished glance with Josh.

'It's not that we won't tell you the truth, Mrs Grey,' Josh said gently. 'We don't know the truth yet. As soon as we do, we'll tell you everything.'

'So tell me what you do know.'

Josh let out his breath slowly. 'I know he's sick. I know his glands are up all over his body. I know he appears anaemic, that he's tired and listless, that he's suffering from a persistent fever and intractible infection of the tonsils. He's pale, he's got a lot of bruises, he's had headaches, he's got an enlarged liver and spleen——'

'And those are the symptoms of leukaemia.'

'They may be, some of them, yes. Only the blood test will give us a definite answer, because all of them could also be explained by glandular fever and tonsillitis combined. Of the two, that's my bet.'

'But he's been tested for glandular fever.'

Josh nodded. 'Quite possibly. We've tested him again, but it may not be conclusive. It often comes back negative, especially in the early days. It's like a pregnancy test. Positive means you are, negative means you might be. Because of that we're also screening for the changes in his blood that might indicate leukaemia, just so we can eliminate it and set your mind at rest.'

She was silent for a while, then her shoulders squared. 'So we still don't know anything for sure.'

'No.'

'When do you expect the results?'

Josh glanced at his watch. 'The first ones, fairly soon. Half an hour, perhaps? Would you like me to ring the lab and ask them?'

She nodded. 'Would you mind? And could I ring my husband? I need to talk to him.'

'Of course—use this phone,' Melissa said instantly, and they left her to it for a moment while Melissa made Mrs Grey a cup of tea and Josh rang the lab and chivvied them for results, then set the phone down with a thoughtful grunt.

The test for glandular fever, the staining for the Epstein-Barr virus, was positive and the indicators of leukaemia were either missing or inconclusive.

However, Josh still wasn't reassured. The boy was sick—too sick for glandular fever alone.

'I know he hasn't got leukaemia,' Josh said quietly to Melissa. 'I just don't know what the hell else it could be. Those bruises worry me. I'm going to talk to him again.'

Melissa went with him, and listened as he patiently questioned the little lad about the bruises.

He was reluctant to tell them in front of his mother, but in the end admitted he had fallen trying to look on top of the kitchen cupboards for his birthday present. It was his birthday in four days' time, and he had been sure the present would be up there.

He had slipped and fallen, jarring himself against the table as he did so and banging his left side.

Melissa watched Josh's face, trying to read his mind. As the boy spoke she could almost hear the cogs turning in his mind, and in hers, too. The trouble was, the only thing she could think of was a ruptured spleen, but that surely would have killed him hours ago. . .

Josh glanced at his watch. 'I'm going to contact Dr Barrett,' he told Mrs Grey. 'I'm wondering if he might have injured himself in the fall yesterday, which might explain this sudden serious deterioration. Could you stay around for a few minutes?'

'Of course,' she agreed, and Josh and Melissa went back into the office.

'Spleen?' she suggested, and he nodded.

'I think he's ruptured it, just very slightly, and because the membrane's still intact, the bleeding's encapsulated and so he's managed to survive. However, I think his time's running out fast. I'm going to contact Andrew, and arrange a scanner to come up to the ward—I don't want him moved more than absolutely necessary. I also want a surgeon here to look at the scanner results. Who would it be today?'

Melissa checked the duty list. 'Ross Hamilton's team. Tom Russell's his SR.'

Josh nodded. 'Get Tom down here to look at him, could you? I'll mobilise the scanner.'

An hour later the scanner had confirmed Josh's fears, and Toby had been whisked off to Theatre for an emergency splenectomy.

By the time Melissa went off duty their little patient was back in the ward, undergoing blood transfusions and hopefully out of danger.

'It was a tiny, tiny split,' Tom Russell told them. 'Really unfortunate, but the thing was so incredibly fragile there was no possibility of repair. Shame, really, but he'll be OK now. It's a good job the membrane held, or he would have died in the night without fail.'

The Greys were shaken but extremely relieved that their son was going to be all right, but the emotion was too much for Mrs Grey and she burst into tears of relief, burying her face in her hands and sobbing uncontrollably.

When she finally pulled herself together she explained that she had lost a sister with leukaemia at a similar age.

'I'm sorry to be so emotional, but it was just too terrifyingly possible for comfort,' she said wanly, 'and then to find out it wasn't that but something that actually came very much nearer to killing him—well, it's a bit much to cope with.'

'I'm sure,' Melissa said understandingly. 'Well, at least you know he's going to be all right.'

As Josh and Melissa left the boy's bedside, Mrs Grey laid her hand on Josh's arm. 'Thank you for not dismissing my fears,' she said quietly.

Josh laid his hand over hers and squeezed gently. 'How could I? You were right, he was seriously ill. I agreed with you—the only difference was the diagnosis and the outcome, and fortunately I was the one who was right,' he told her with a smile. His eyes swung round to the boy in the bed. 'He'll be fine in a few days. You'll see a huge improvement in him now.'

Josh walked back to the work station with Melissa, the smile lingering on his face, and as they turned the corner he winked at her.

'How's about that for brilliance?' he grinned.

She rolled her eyes. 'What's it like to be perfect?'

'Oh—I just accept it as my lot in life,' he said with a straight face, but his eyes danced with mischief.

'I'll bet you were teacher's pet,' she accused, her eyes narrowing.

'Me?' He chuckled. 'No way. I was too busy putting lizards in her desk.'

'I can well believe it,' Melissa said drily. 'Now I think about it, you were probably too damn clever to be good all the time.'

'That's me,' he said with a grin, and, chucking her under the chin, he strode off down the corridor, hands in his pockets, whistling cheerfully to himself.

'Tricky one, that spleen. He's a clever guy,' Anna said behind her.

'Yes.'

'Wonder if it'll be passed on to the baby?'

Melissa turned and looked at Anna. 'That subject——' she began.

'Is definitely taboo. Sorry. Going for tea?'

Melissa smiled at her. 'No, I'm going home to have a hot bath, a big meal and an evening in front of the television. I feel like celebrating for Toby.'

And for me, she added silently, because my baby's father is a man to be proud of.

What a crying shame she couldn't believe in happy ever after. . .

While her time at work with Josh was interesting and busy and blessed with sunshine and laughter, by contrast her evenings and weekends were almost frighteningly empty and quiet.

She was preparing for the baby's arrival, knitting small jackets and colourful stripy socks, and that night she settled in front of the television with a pile of little pieces and started sewing them together.

It grew dark, but she didn't bother to shut the curtains. She only had a little more to do before she had finished the jacket. . .

There was a sound outside, a slight scraping noise.

Curious, she went into the kitchen without turning on the light, and stood listening.

Just outside the door she could hear something that sounded like—breathing? Her flesh felt cold, the little hairs standing up all over her arms and legs, and her tongue flicked out to moisten her dry lips.

What was it? Who was it?

The bolt was on the door, but as she watched the old-fashioned latch lifted and rattled.

Fear streamed through her like ice, and, running for the stairs, she fled into her bedroom, slammed and locked the door and phoned the hospital. 'Get me Josh Lancaster,' she whispered urgently. Seconds later she was put through to him, and she could have wept with relief. 'Josh? Help—there's someone trying to get into my cottage!' she said frantically. 'You've got to come—please, help me!'

'Call the police—I'll be right there,' he promised, and the phone went dead.

Terrified at the loss of contact she dialled 999, gave the police her address and directions, and then hid in the wardrobe. It wouldn't hold the intruder up for long, but at least it would give her a few seconds more.

'Oh, God, please, let them get here soon. . .'

Josh parked a little way down the lane, sprinted down the verge silently and crept into the garden. It was almost pitch-black, the moon hidden behind the clouds, and he gave his eyes a moment to adjust.

The doors and windows all seemed secure still, and he could hear something moving in the shrubbery under the windows. Just then the moon emerged from behind the clouds and he could just make out a shadowy form. As he started to cross the lawn the sound of sirens and the spray of red and blue lights swamped the area.

Within seconds he found himself face down on the ground under two burly policemen, handcuffs being slapped on his wrists.

'Get off me,' he growled. 'For God's sake, I'm a friend of hers! She called me——'

'A likely story,' one of the policemen said drily. 'Why don't you just get up and come along quietly with us, son?'

'I would get up if I could,' he grumbled, and then the pressure eased and he was yanked to his feet.

'Right, young man, I'm arresting you for loitering with intent——'

'Oh, for heaven's sake——' he began, but the policeman in charge fixed him with a beady eye and advised him that he didn't have to say anything, but what he did say might be taken down and used in evidence, then went and banged on the door.

'Police, madam. You can come out now; we've found your intruder.'

A moment later the door inched open, and Melissa's frightened face appeared in the doorway.

'Josh?' she said in astonishment. 'Why have you got handcuffs on?'

He sighed. 'I've been arrested.'

'What? What for?'

'Loitering with intent, madam,' the policeman informed her.

'Loitering—but he was at work! I called him. It can't be him!'

'Well, if he isn't your intruder, then where is the bloke?' the policeman asked, clearly getting puzzled.

'There,' Josh said calmly, tilting his head towards her shrubbery. 'There's your intruder—eating the flowers.'

They swung a flashlight in the direction Josh was indicating, and there in the middle of her little shrubbery was a goat, happily munching on a fuchsia.

Melissa, the whole thing too much for her, sagged against the doorpost and started to giggle helplessly.

'Oh, Molly! You gave me such a fright! You naughty goat!'

Molly swung her head towards Melissa, said, 'Bleaagh,' and carried on eating the fuchsia. The policemen, somewhat embarrassed, released Josh and went off with the goat in tow to find the unfortunate animal's owner, leaving them alone in the cottage.

'I think I deserve a cup of coffee, at least, for my part in that,' Josh said, brushing his front down to remove the grass crushed into his sweatshirt.

'So do I—thank you for coming so promptly. . .how did you get here, by the way? I didn't see your car.'

'I parked up the road so as not to alarm your intruder,' Josh told her drily.

She giggled again, and he glared at her.

'How about a bit of sympathy here?' he grumbled. 'Or even an apology, if you're feeling that generous.'

'I'm sorry he arrested you,' she said, trying hard to keep a straight face.

'*You're* sorry? I was squashed into the grass by two extremely large men—I don't think my ribs will ever be the same again.'

He looked at her, then with an exasperated sigh he tugged her into his arms. 'Come here, silly girl. Are you OK?'

She nodded, then to her horror her eyes filled with tears. 'I know it's crazy but I was scared—I don't think I've ever been so scared in my life. When the latch lifted——'

She shook her head, buried it in his chest and breathed deeply. She could smell the crushed grass, and earth, and under it the faint tang of that mysterious aftershave. His arms tightened fractionally, then he let go with one, keeping the other firmly round her shoulders, and led her through into the sitting-room.

'I'll shut the curtains, we'll have a drink and then you can lock up behind me. All right?'

He disappeared to make the coffee, leaving her alone. The curtains were closed, the lights were on and she could hear him in the next room, but somehow she was still afraid. She needed the loo, but the thought of going upstairs on her own——

'What's the matter?' he asked softly.

She chewed her lip and didn't answer. It seemed too ridiculous for words. After all, it was only a goat——

'Are you scared?'

His voice was warm and gentle and reassuring. She nodded, swallowing the huge lump that lurked in her throat. It came back again straight away, and to her disgust her eyes filled again.

'Oh, sweetheart,' he murmured, and, sitting on the arm of the chair, he wrapped his arms round her and rocked her gently against his chest.

It felt so good. She didn't want him to move, but the kettle clicked and he stood up and held out his hand, taking her with him into the kitchen while he made the coffee.

'I need the loo,' she mumbled, and without questioning it he led her upstairs and waited just outside the door until she emerged. 'It's so silly,' she began, but he hugged her.

'Rubbish. You had a hell of a fright—it could have been anyone. You need outside lights that come on automatically, and a guard dog so you feel safe.'

'Calico hates dogs,' she told him. 'I'll be fine; I'm just making a fuss about nothing.'

But she sat beside him on the settee, her feet snuggled under his thigh, and when he set his coffee-cup down and glanced at his watch her heart sank.

'You go up to bed—I'll sleep here,' he told her.

She eyed the settee sceptically. 'I don't think you will—not much, anyway. I'll be all right. You go home.'

But he pushed her towards the stairs, took the quilt and pillows she gave him from the airing cupboard and went back down.

She was all right at first, with her door open and listening to the quiet sound of the television as he watched the late night news.

It was later, when she woke from a dream with her heart pounding and a scream in her throat, that everything fell apart.

In seconds Josh was in the doorway. 'Lissa?' he murmured, his voice gruff with sleep. 'It's OK, sweetheart. I'm here. Go back to sleep.'

She sat bolt upright in the bed, her body trembling. 'I had a dream,' she told him. 'The latch was lifting, and then the door started to open and I woke up. . .'

The mattress gave under his weight, and then his arms were round her, cradling her against his chest. 'Lie down and go back to sleep,' he coaxed, and she snuggled down into the hollow of his shoulder, wrapped firmly against his side, and gradually the terror left her.

She couldn't sleep, though. His scent was too disturbing, the warmth of his body against hers, the beat of his heart under her hand calling to her. He was still fully dressed, and her hand itched to feel the hard, broad strength of his chest naked beneath her palm.

She tipped her head back so she could look at him, and in the little spill of light from the landing she could see his eyes watching her.

'Lissa?' he breathed, and then his mouth found hers and she was lost.

The kiss seemed endless, the heat of his mouth warming the cold, empty recesses of her heart, and with a little cry she brought her hands up and cradled his face, loving the harsh texture of his stubble against her palms, the warmth of his skin, the hard strength of his jaw.

He moved away, and in the half-light she could see him stripping off his clothes, throwing them anywhere.

Then he turned back the covers, sat her up and peeled her nightie over her head. He didn't bother to cover them again, instead exploring the changed textures and planes of her body with his hands and lips.

She could see his face, the jaw clenched, his eyes glittering with the fever of desire as he ran his hand over the smooth swell of their child and down, brushing the soft, sensitive skin of her thighs.

'Lovely—so lovely,' he whispered, his breath playing over her skin, driving her wild.

His hands were bolder now, parting her, teasing her, and his lips followed, stealing untold intimacies. She started to shake, her body's response swamping her, and with a low moan she reached out for him and drew him into her arms.

'Please, Josh,' she begged, and with a shuddering sigh he slid deep into her. A convulsion gripped her, then another, and suddenly, without warning, the whole world seemed to fall in on her and she cried out his name.

She felt his arms tighten, holding her hard against his chest, and then he stiffened, sweat breaking out on his heated skin, and with a harsh groan he fell against her, dropping his head into the hollow of her shoulder and whispering her name as the violent shudders of release racked his body.

Then he lifted his head and kissed her, oh, so tenderly, and said, 'I love you, Lissa.'

Biting her lips to hold back the words, she felt a huge sadness well up inside her.

Damn him. Why had he done that? Why had he gone and made her love him?

Pain swamped her, the tears falling just to spite her, and then, the greatest irony of all, Josh cradled her against his chest and comforted her in her desperation.

She was up and dressed in the morning before he was even awake. When he came down, a wary look on his face, she was primed and ready.

'You took advantage of me,' she accused him before his foot was even off the bottom step.

He watched her assessingly. 'Don't ask me to apologise,' he warned. 'I'd do it again any time. We're right together, Lissa, you and I. We should be together.'

'No. I told you, Josh—I don't want a relationship and I won't have one——'

'Well, what the hell was that last night?' he asked in amazement. 'Are you going to let just anybody do those things to you!'

She turned away. She couldn't look at him and

remember all the things he had done, the intimacies she had allowed him——

Hot colour burned her cheeks. 'Don't be ridiculous,' she snapped. 'You sneaked under my guard—caught me without any defences.'

'So I could have been anyone.'

'No!'

'Well, then,' he continued reasonably, 'that must mean we have a relationship.'

'Well, of course we do!' she exclaimed, turning on him. 'I know that. I just don't *want* one!'

He was silent for a while, then with a shrug he went into the kitchen. 'Breakfast?' he said.

'I've had mine. I'm going to work, and I'd like to lock up the cottage.'

He came back out of the kitchen, propping himself on the doorframe.

'Are you by any chance throwing me out?' he said mildly.

His gentle scrutiny made her feel like a shrew, but she had to stick to her guns. She had no defences against this man, none at all. It was no good weakening now, before they were even over the first hurdle!

'Yes,' she said flatly. 'I am—and I don't think it would be a good idea for you to come back, either. I can't trust you, Josh.'

'Or yourself with me.'

His eyes were steady, not accusing, but seeing too much. 'Just go, please,' she said as calmly as she could manage.

'Right.' He scooped up his shoes, wriggled his feet into them and headed for the door. 'By the way,' he threw over his shoulder, 'I've lost a sock. Can you let me have it back when you find it?'

And then he was gone, leaving her alone.

Except she wasn't. The house was full of reminders

of him—the bedding folded neatly now on the settee, the sheets upstairs in a wild tangle——

She went up, stripped the bed and marched down, shoving the offending bedding into the washing-machine.

No *way* could she sleep with the scent of their loving clinging to the sheets and wrapping her around in a haze of memories.

If only it was so easy to wash the memories away. . .

CHAPTER SIX

UNTIL that point it had been easy to work with Josh—
so easy that Melissa hadn't realised how effectively
he'd wormed his way under her guard and sneaked
into her heart.

She still couldn't trust him. She might love him, she
might want him—well, no might about it, she *did* both
love him and want him—but that didn't mean it would
last, on his part anyway. He only wanted her for the
baby. She was sure of that, whatever he said to the
contrary. His lovemaking last night had amply demonstrated that, with those tender, almost reverent kisses
he had laid on her skin over the gentle swell of
their child.

At one point it had kicked, and a wondrous smile
had brushed his eyes. 'Hello, baby,' he'd murmured,
and she had felt an irrational pang of jealousy.

For now, she and the baby were inextricably linked,
but what would happen when that was no longer
so and he grew bored with her? She was older than
him, four years older. In a few years she'd be enter-
ing middle age, and he'd still be quite definitely
in his prime. How would he cope when she lost her
figure, the natural elasticity of her skin, her grace
of movement? Would he cast her aside in favour of
some bright young thing with stars in her eyes and
masses of sexual energy? If he even stayed around
that long.

They saw so many children whose parents were divorced, squabbling over the bedside and tearing the kids
to pieces. No way was that happening to her baby.

She had found divorce traumatic enough when it was just her, and she could reason and understand and make some kind of sense of it.

How could a child be expected to cope with that?

Because it would happen. She knew very well she couldn't hold him. She was all right now, because the buffeting effect of her hormones was protecting her from the awful pain of her illness, but what about when the baby was born and the symptoms returned? How would he cope with that? And if she needed a hysterectomy, so there was no possibility of any further children?

That was a body-blow most male egos couldn't handle. Would he be able to?

No. Their relationship would fall apart, tearing the baby to pieces, shredding up her home yet again—she couldn't face it, couldn't risk it.

And yet still she loved him.

Well, that was simply her cross to bear. Everybody had one. Hers was called Josh Lancaster.

She arrived at work dreading facing him again, but he was doing a clinic and hardly appeared on the ward all day. He seemed a little distant and remote, and the stupid, sentimental and easily led part of her that loved him grieved for the comfortable relationship they had lost.

Toby Grey's mother regarded her thoughtfully as she did his drugs, and said quietly, 'You look very tired. Are you all right, Sister?'

She forced a smile. No, she wouldn't cry. 'Yes, I'm fine. I didn't have a very good night.'

Liar! her conscience screamed, and her cheeks heated spontaneously. She busied herself with the drugs trolley, checking dosages against the chart and with Anna Long, and as they moved on Anna said, 'OK, I know the subject of Josh is taboo, but she's right—you look bloody awful. If you want to talk to someone, I'm always there.'

Another person who was there for her was Jo Carter, the gynaecologist she had been seeing before her pregnancy. Later that day she gave her a call and arranged to see her for an antenatal check. Technically she was under Alex, Jo's husband, but, even though Jo wasn't on his obstetrics team and only did gynae now, they had agreed Jo should follow the pregnancy through until the time of delivery.

'How's it going?' Jo asked her on the phone now.

'Oh—OK. I'm tired.'

There was a pause, then Jo said, 'Forgive me for interfering, but I heard a rumour. . .'

Melissa sighed. 'Well, surprise, surprise. If you're waiting for wedding bells, I shouldn't hold your breath. I'll see you tomorrow.'

She cut the connection, frowned at the phone and wondered how Jo had heard.

Jungle drums, she decided. After all, it was difficult to imagine how it could possibly remain a secret with his standing on the ward and saying quite clearly, 'That's my baby!'

No doubt they all thought it was desperately romantic, his following her up from London. The blasted hospital was a hotbed of romance. Even Andrew Barrett, the quietest and least romantic man she had ever met, had succumbed a little under two years ago and was now the proud father of a year-old baby girl, with another on the way. She had yet to forgive him for revealing her whereabouts to Josh so casually. Clearly he was another closet romantic, she thought in disgust. If only he'd said something to her, she could have— what? Run away?

Just because Andrew had found happiness, she thought, he had to go and turn Cupid, not content with his own wife and family. Cross as she was, though, she couldn't deny him his happiness. He deserved a family, because he was a thoroughly nice man and wonderful with the children.

Like Josh, her conscience pricked, but she squashed the thought. He was too sexy, too confident, too plain gorgeous to trust, and if they were all hoping for a happy ending they were going to be doomed to disappointment.

She closed her mind to the knotty problem of Josh, and went to see how Toby Grey was faring after his op the day before. He was still on hourly obs, and every now and then Melissa herself checked him just to be on the safe side.

Even in his drowsy and sedated condition, though, it was easy to see he was in better shape than he had been twenty-four hours before.

She smiled down at him, and he managed a weak little grin in return. 'How's your tum?' she asked.

'Sore,' he croaked, 'and my mouth's horrid.'

She nodded. 'It will be. We'll give you something for the pain in a little while, and your mum can give you a mouthwash to make you feel fresher. In the meantime I just want to empty your stomach again so it doesn't press on the sore bit, OK?'

She fitted the syringe to the end of the nasogastric tube and aspirated his stomach contents, measuring the quantity and checking that all was normal.

'There isn't so much this time, so it looks as though his system's starting to work again,' she told Mrs Grey. 'That means he'll be able to have the tube out soon—that'll be nice, won't it?'

She ruffled the little boy's hair, and he smiled, clearly pleased at the thought of losing the uncomfortable tube in his nose.

Melissa checked the wound drain, nodded in satisfaction over the clean suture line and covered him up again. 'Soon have you on the mend, won't we? Would you like a television on your bedside table later?'

He nodded. 'Maybe. I'm a bit sleepy.'

'OK. We'll leave it till tomorrow, all right?'

She left him to sleep, and suggested to his mother that she might like to take a stroll down to the canteen and have some tea. 'He'll be fine; we'll keep an eye on him,' she promised, and so Mrs Grey went off for a much-needed break.

Melissa, on the other hand, was rushed off her feet. They had an emergency admission through A and E, a child who had fallen off his bike and was suffering concussion, and just to be perverse the post-op children were all sick one after the other, with the inevitable sheet-changing and clearing up that went with it.

The nursing staff were spread pretty thin on the ground that day, with all the calls on their time, and when the older kids started to play up Melissa was ready to murder them.

Emotion, lack of sleep and general exhaustion eroded her temper at the speed of light, but it must have shown because when she walked into that area of the ward the hush was immediate.

She didn't have to say a word, just looked at them, shook her head and turned off the television.

'Hey, we were watching that!' one boy called.

'You were?' she said sceptically. 'When I came in, you were chucking your pillows about. Now pick them up, put them back and settle down before I split you all up. And as for you, Simon, you needn't sit there and look innocent. I know quite well you were up on your feet again. Now get back into bed and stay there. There's plenty of room in the adult orthopaedic ward for you, young man, and believe me, they won't take kindly to your antics. If necessary we'll put you in traction. That should sort you out. Now just behave, all of you, or the television goes off again and stays off.'

She turned the set back on, and, with a bit of fidgeting and grumbling about the channel, they settled down.

Things were better after that, but she was still more than ready to go home by the end of the day. Her shift finally ended and, the ward handed over, she drove tiredly home.

Swinging on to her drive with casual familiarity, her eyes widened and she slammed on her brakes, coming to an immediate and rather undignified halt in a slither of gravel.

There was a caravan on the drive—a huge, ugly, washed-out green monstrosity with a pea-green stripe round its waist, and moss growing in the gutters. Josh's car was parked on the lane outside, and there was just room for hers in front of the caravan.

Parking it, she got out, slammed the door and marched up to the green monstrosity.

The door swung open as she approached, and Josh stood there, wiping his hands on a tea-towel, eyeing her warily.

As well he might, she thought crossly.

'I hope you've got a pretty damn good explanation,' she snapped, glaring at him.

He shrugged, and came down the steps so that her head wasn't cranked back at such an angle. She wanted to get on to the bottom step so she could glare straight into his eyes, but she refused to give in to such a childish impulse.

'Think of it as a kennel,' he said obscurely.

'A kennel?' she exclaimed. 'How on earth is this humungous monstrosity a *kennel*?'

'For your guard dog.'

'But I don't have a guard dog,' she said emphatically.

'And furthermore, I don't want one——'

'Tough, because I just volunteered.'

She stared at him in astonishment. 'You? You did what? You seriously imagine I'm going to allow you to leave that disgusting heap here on my drive and actually *live in it*?' Her voice was getting shriller, and she clamped down hard and forced it to lower to more civilised and reasonable tones. 'Josh, I really don't think you've thought this through——'

'On the contrary, I've been thinking about it for ages. Last night just finished it for me. I worry about you, Lissa.' He reached out and smoothed back her hair, and she slapped his hand away and stepped back out of reach.

'I don't need you to protect me,' she told him firmly. 'I was fine last night.'

His smile was gently teasing. 'Is that why you wouldn't even go to the loo alone?'

She couldn't answer that, so she huffed instead. His smile widened.

'Silly girl. Just let me live here and keep an eye on you. I won't get in your way——'

'You aren't coming in,' she warned, backing down a little because in fact the thought of him just in hailing distance was growing on her by the minute. 'You can't use the bathroom—there's an outside loo you can use, but that's all. Not the kitchen, and no creeping round me in the evening to watch the television.'

He chuckled. 'Don't panic, Lissa. I've got a television, and a kitchen, and a stereo system and a shower and everything I could possibly need. The loo I will use—thank you for your generosity. Otherwise, if I could have some power through an extension lead, my happiness will be complete.'

She humphed. 'I suppose you've even got one.'

He reached into the caravan and brought out a

brightly coloured spool of cable. 'Perhaps you'd be so kind as to plug it in for me?' he suggested.

He handed it in to her through a little window, and she managed to secure it even with the cable in the way so that it was intruder-proof. Then she went into the kitchen and started to make a cup of tea—just one. He could make his own. If he thought he was scrounging off her——

There was a tap on her door, and she yanked it open. 'I said you weren't coming in——'

'I didn't want to. I came to ask if you'd like to join me for a cup of tea.'

Guilt swamped her, but she battled it down. 'No, thank you, I've just made one,' she lied, and shut the door in his face. Damn. How did he do it? Turn the tables on her like that time after time after time? Wretched man.

She pulled the sheets out of the washing-machine, hung them on the line and then, taking her cup of tea, she settled down on the settee—in *her* corner—and watched the door of the caravan.

What was he doing in there? He had carried a load of stuff in from the car, and now he was doing something inside. Unpacking, probably. Settling in. She sighed. A moment later he appeared, a large plastic container in hand, and pointed at her outside tap questioningly.

'Of course you can have water,' she yelled waspishly, and scowled at his knowing smile. Damn the man, he was winding her up to the limit, wringing every last ounce out of the situation. She leant her head back against the wing of the settee and caught a whiff of his aftershave on the upholstery.

Memories flooded her, and with an impotent little scream she moved to the chair. She could hear him outside, filling the water container. How was she supposed to ignore him and learn to live without him if he was here, hanging around offering her cups of tea and looking devastatingly sexy in those obscene, threadbare jeans of his?

His back came into view, legs braced under the weight of the water container, the faded denim stretched taut over those wonderful legs and firm, neat buttocks——

With a little growl of frustration she shut her eyes and sighed.

He was impossible. Having him here was impossible. The whole damn situation was impossible.

Still, it was September now. Soon it would be cold. One good, hard frost and she'd be able to send him packing.

Or die in the attempt.

Josh filled the kettle, lit the gas burner under it and sprawled out full-length on the bed to wait for the water to boil. It was a lovely evening, mild and tranquil, the birdsong all around filling him with peace.

He was quite at home in the caravan. As the oldest of six children, he had often taken refuge in it on trips home during the holidays, and it had always represented a peaceful oasis, away from bustle and strain and the difficult demands of the real world.

His father had brought it over without demanding a word of explanation, and inside it there was a big fruit cake and an apple pie from his mother.

He would have some fruit cake with his cup of tea in a minute, but just now he was happy doing nothing.

Well, not exactly nothing. Watching, really. He could see the cottage from his window and as he lay there a light came on in the sitting-room and Lissa walked across to the kitchen, one hand resting on the gentle swell of her abdomen.

His child. Lord, it had been something else last night making love to her. He hadn't ever doubted that he would still want to while she was pregnant. What had stunned him was how beautiful she had been with her body ripening with her advancing pregnancy, and how much more it had meant this time. Whether it was because of the baby or just because he knew and loved her more, he didn't know. probably both. Whatever, it had shattered him to realise how much he needed her. And need her he had, both emotionally and physically.

He shifted, his jeans uncomfortably tight with the memory, and watched as she came back from the kitchen with a plate in her hand.

She didn't sit at the table but curled up on the settee, in his corner, and turned the television on with the remote control. He watched her eat, felt a sharp stab of desire when she flicked out her tongue to chase a stray grain of rice on her top lip, and when she set the plate down and tucked up her legs under her he was treated to a startling flash of milk-white thigh.

He closed his eyes and groaned. His jeans were going to burst in a moment, watching her.

Damn. He turned on the television, made a cup of coffee and slouched back in the corner. Not even the fruit cake tempted him. He couldn't be bothered to eat. Watching Lissa was all the sustenance he needed.

She was knitting now, tiny little white things that looked impossibly small. The television couldn't hold his attention, and suddenly he just had to talk to her.

He picked up his new mobile phone and dialled her number, then watched as she reached out one long, graceful arm and scooped up the receiver.

'Hello?' Her voice was breathy and impossibly sexy, and his jeans groaned again under the strain.

'Hi.' He cleared his throat. 'It's Josh. I just thought

I'd let you have my mobile number in case you need to get hold of me,' he improvised.

She peered out of the window at the caravan. It was in darkness still. He could watch her better that way.

'Where are you?' she asked.

'In the caravan.'

'There aren't any lights on.'

He reached overhead and flicked a switch, and his view of her was instantly dimmed.

He waved, and she waved back, then pulled a cross little face and glared at him, ramming her hand into her lap to keep it out of mischief. He smiled. She was trying so hard to cut him out, but he wouldn't let her. He didn't intend to lose her so easily again. She looked away, clearly frustrated.

'Well?' she snapped down the phone. 'What is it?'

Josh was miles away. 'What's what?'

'The number! That's why you rang, remember?'

'Ah.' Belatedly he remembered his excuse for phoning her, and glanced down at the leaflet he had been given with the phone. 'Here it is.' He dictated it to her, watching as she wrote it down, the tip of her tongue caught in the corner of her mouth in concentration.

She always did that. He wondered idly if she had any idea how wild it drove him.

'Right. Thanks. Not that I expect to need it.'

'Of course not. But I'm here if you need me. Remember that.'

There was a pause for a moment, then a murmured, 'Thanks, Josh,' before she set the phone down.

He watched as she got up and closed the curtains, shutting her off from his view.

He felt suddenly unbelievably lonely.

*　　*　　*

Melissa woke to a view of the caravan from her bedroom window. It was the last thing she had seen last night, and the first thing she saw this morning.

It annoyed her.

She conveniently forgot how glad she had been when she had woken in the night and remembered he was there, phone by his side, able to hear her screams if necessary.

She tugged on her uniform, noting almost absently how tight the dress was getting now. She had bought a new one which she had hoped would see her through, but now she wasn't so sure. She still had five weeks to go at work, and the rate she was growing she would need at least one size up, if not more.

Still, it might come in handy when she went back to work, if she hadn't got her figure back.

He wouldn't want her then, she was sure, with her saggy, stretch-marked stomach and droopy breasts.

Oh, well.

Depressed by the thought, she ate a piece of toast that was only slightly burnt, washed it down with a cup of tea and went out to her car.

Josh was just emerging from the caravan, wearing only a pair of jeans with the snap undone and looking altogether too gorgeous for her peace of mind.

'Morning,' he growled in that deliciously sexy early-morning voice of his.

'Good morning,' she said, conscious of the warmth of her cheeks and so sounding a little prim. 'Lovely day.'

He grinned. 'It is, isn't it? Wonder if it'll rain later. Then again, of course, it might snow for Christmas. What do you suppose the chances are?'

She got into her car and slammed the door shut. Infuriating man. She was only trying to make polite conversation.

She reversed off the drive, turned and drove away, refusing to allow herself even to glance in the rear-view mirror. Well, perhaps a tiny one——

He waved, but she ignored him and forced herself to think of other things—the baby, for instance.

She was seeing Jo Carter today. They would talk about what the future held in view of her current state of health. Maybe she would have something positive to say.

Somehow Melissa doubted it. She didn't get that lucky.

In fact, she saw Jo much earlier, as soon as she arrived on the ward.

Rob, the SHO, was there with Jo and Alex, and they were standing round a bed with rails up, deep in earnest conversation.

She found the night sister and asked what was going on.

'Oh, their little one—Amy. She's got fever and vomiting and seems to have an infected bite—it looks as though she's got septicaemia.'

'Oh, my goodness, poor little scrap. What treatment is she having?'

'Pass,' the sister said. 'They only arrived a few minutes before you. I'll hand over to you and you can go and find out.'

Within minutes she was free to join the group huddled around Amy's bed, and she went straight up to Jo, squeezed her shoulder and smiled at Rob and Alex.

'Ah, Melissa,' Rob said instantly, clearly relieved by her arrival. 'Amy's come in with a twelve-hour history of vomiting, fever and tachycardia following infection in an insect bite which she's scratched. It seems a bit inflamed, and obviously the infection has spread and is poisoning her system. We're not sure yet which organism is responsible, but we're going to put a drip up to rehydrate her and we'll take some blood for culture. In the meantime I suggest we contact Andrew or Josh——'

'I'm here. What's the problem?'

Melissa felt the tension ease out of her. If her appearance was anything to go by Amy was clearly very sick, and her illness was beyond Rob's ability to cope. There were so many things that could go wrong, and so many different treatments. While Rob filled Josh in, Melissa extracted as much information as she could from Jo and Alex.

'She started being sick yesterday evening,' Jo said. 'At first I thought it was something she'd picked up in nursery school, flu or something. Then this morning Alex noticed the bite on her side, and we wondered if that could be the source of the infection.'

Josh was listening to them now, and turned back the sheet to look at the bite. It was certainly angry, but it didn't look bad enough to have caused the child to be this sick.

Her face was flushed, but her hands and feet were cold and mottled, and she looked as if she was going into shock.

Josh spoke gently to her, asking her questions as he gently palpated her abdomen and listened to her chest and tummy.

'She's got no bowel sounds, and I really don't think that bite's bad enough to have made her so ill,' he told Amy's worried parents. 'I want to do a lumbar puncture, and just to be on the safe side we'll treat her for meningococcal septicaemia as well as the possibility of a Staphylococcal infection from the bite.'

Jo's face blanched. 'What?' she whispered. 'Meningococcal? Aren't you over-reacting? She's got a poisoned bite. It must be that.'

He shook his head. 'I don't think so. I hope so, but

I've just got this gut instinct that she's too sick for a Staph infection. Her cry's high pitched, she's turning away from the light, she's going into shock—I'm going to set up the drip and get everything I can think of into her just to be on the safe side before we do the lumbar puncture. I want to get treatment under way as soon as we can.'

Jo and Alex exchanged a glance, and then Alex put his arm round Jo's shoulders and hugged her. 'She'll be all right, darling,' he murmured. 'Don't worry.'

Josh looked from one to the other. 'Would you rather get Andrew's opinion? I won't be in the least offended, but I do think we ought to get on with it and he's not in the hospital yet.'

Alex shook his head. 'Carry on. He trusts you; I've heard him talk about you. You treat her as you think fit.'

Josh nodded briskly, then turned to Melissa. 'We'll have her in the treatment-room. I want a sterile field, and I'd like you to scrub and assist. If I can't get a vein in her arm with the first attempt I'll do a cut-down for a vein in her ankle, but I hope I won't have to because I don't want to mess about. Who's going to hold her for the lumbar puncture?'

'I will,' Alex said calmly, although Melissa could see a muscle ticking in his jaw. The professional doctor was taking over from the anxious father, but the transition wasn't easy.

They went into the treatment-room, and Melissa enlisted Anna's assistance as well in preparing the room as quickly as possible while Josh set up an oxygen mask and tilted the treatment table down at the head end slightly.

The little girl was whimpering, frightened by the strange surroundings and obviously feeling very unwell, and Josh was unable to make her keep the mask on.

'Dr Carter, could you hold it for her just near her face, please?' he asked Jo, and she took the mask, laid her own cheek against Amy's and murmured reassuringly to her as the oxygen played across the little girl's mouth and nose.

Her colour improved slightly, and Josh nodded.

'OK, Amy,' he said in a quiet, very calm voice. 'I just want to put a little plastic tube into your arm so we can make you better, darling.'

'Left arm?' Melissa asked, and he nodded.

'I think so. I can get to it easiest. Mr Carter, if you could hold it steady?'

Alex grasped her arm, they put a band round it to compress the vessels to help the vein to stand up, and then Josh swabbed the site, gripped her hand firmly and slid the needle in.

Amy screamed, jerked her arm and Josh immediately withdrew the needle.

'Damn. Missed it. I'll have one more go—it looks fairly good.'

Amy, however, was unimpressed.

'No!' she screamed. 'I don't want a plastic tube! Mummy, no!'

Jo put her arms round her, cuddling the child up against her chest, and turned imploring eyes to Josh. 'Do you have to?' she asked softly.

'Dr Carter, you know I do,' he told her, and she nodded.

'Amy, sweetheart, just one more try, please?'

'No, I don't want to!' she screamed.

Josh shook his head slowly. 'I'm sorry, we have to. We haven't got time to mess about. I'll do it as quickly as I can.'

Again Amy screamed, but they didn't give her a

chance to struggle this time and the line was in and taped down very quickly indeed.

'Right. I want samples for haemoglobin, white cells and platelet counts, culture, electrolytes and urea,' Josh rapped out while Jo cuddled the sobbing child and Alex smoothed her hair back, his jaw working steadily.

Melissa counted out the bottles, warmed the culture sample bottles in readiness and then filled and labelled them from the full syringe Josh passed her.

'Right. Fluids, benzylpencillin and cloxacillin stat, I think, Melissa. She'd better have plasma. Get some fresh frozen plasma up from Haematology fast, please. Anna, could you ring?'

Anna disappeared, and Melissa labelled the last bottle while Josh set up the saline drip to counter shock and to rehydrate her, and while he established her normal weight and calculated the volume of plasma she would require, Melissa got the drugs trolley, drew up the stat doses of antibiotic and handed the syringes to Anna for checking.

Once they were injected into Amy via the drip, Josh sat back and let out a long, slow sigh.

'Right. Are you ready for the lumbar puncture?'

Amy's parents sighed, nodded and prepared Amy for yet another distressing procedure while Melissa and Josh prepared the equipment.

Then Alex turned Amy on her side, and curved her round, one arm round her neck, the other hooked behind her knees, until her spine was flexed.

Josh injected a local anaesthetic around the entry site for the lumbar tap, and Amy cried and tried to wriggle, but Alex held her firmly, Jo cuddled her head and after a few moments Josh tested the site to see if she reacted.

'OK, it's gone. Are you ready?' he asked, and then

with great care and ridiculous ease he inserted the huge needle between her vertebrae and into the space around the spinal cord. She screamed again, fighting Alex, but he held her steady even though his face was chalk-white and he had to close his eyes.

'OK, I'm in,' Josh murmured. The first thing he did was measure the pressure; then he examined the cerebrospinal fluid for blood. 'Good, it's a clean specimen,' he muttered, and, releasing the tap, he allowed a sample to run off into the bottle Melissa held out to him.

The sample collected, he withdrew the needle, swabbed the site and covered it, and Alex released the sobbing, unhappy little girl.

'All done, Amy—good girl, well done,' Josh said reassuringly. 'Right. Now we can watch and see what happens. Hopefully she should begin to show an almost immediate improvement. Can we get those samples off to the lab?'

Melissa nodded. 'Alvin was passing—I told him to wait. He's taking them straight down.'

'Is he reliable?'

'Alvin?' Melissa smiled reassuringly. 'Alvin's the world's most reliable man. It's a shame all hospital porters aren't modelled on him.'

'Good. Right, let's get this young lady back into the ward and settle down in a quiet corner—do we have a single room at the moment?'

Melissa nodded. 'We soon can have. Anna, could you move Lucy out? I think she's feeling much better and she's a bit bored now. Put her with the monsters.'

'The monsters?' Jo and Alex said together.

Melissa grinned. 'The older kids at the end. They're the pits. One in particular, Simon, I am more than ready to send home but he's in for long-term orthopaedic work after smashing up his legs in a car accident and unfortunately we're all stuck with each other for another few weeks!'

'Withdraw his pain relief,' Josh said drily. 'That should settle him down.'

Melissa laughed. 'Don't worry, it's been suggested.' She turned to the little child on the treatment table. 'Right, Amy, my lovely,' she murmured, 'let's find you a nice, quiet room where you can go to sleep, OK? You've been such a good girl. It's all over now.' She smoothed back the damp hair that was clinging in little ringlets round her tragic little face, and Amy's eyes drooped.

'She's shattered,' Jo said. 'We've been up all night with her.'

'I'm sure. Josh, do you want to take a swab from this bite?'

He nodded. 'When it bursts. Don't mess her about any more now.'

Just then the door swung open and Andrew came in. 'Jo, Alex, I just heard. How is she?'

'Ill,' Alex said economically. 'Josh has done a lumbar tap and is treating her for meningococcal septicaemia.'

Andrew's eyes swivelled to Josh. 'Really?'

Josh nodded. 'I just had a feeling——'

'She's got a rash,' Jo said quietly. 'Look—it's just come up all over her. A classic meningococcal rash.' She looked at Josh. 'I'm sorry I doubted you.'

Josh lifted his hands in a dismissive gesture. 'It was just a gut feeling. I'm glad I went with it.'

'Has she had benzylpenicillin?' Andrew asked urgently.

Josh nodded. 'And cloxacillin, in case it was Staphylococcus. We've sent blood and CSF to the lab for testing. The results should confirm it.'

Anna came back in and told them the room was ready, and they moved the three-year-old into the less threatening environment, settled her down for a rest and found a couple of pillows for Jo, so she could make herself comfy in the chair beside her daughter.

'Now,' Anna said while Andrew and Josh conferred over the case and its continuing management, 'can I get you two a cup of tea?'

'Oh, I'd love one,' Jo said wearily.

Alex shook his head. 'I can't—I'm already late for my clinic and I've got a ward round to do first. I'll be up later.'

He kissed his wife and his daughter, thanked the ward staff again and strode off in the direction of the corridor, checking his watch again.

'He hates keeping people waiting,' Jo said softly. 'He always tries to work to time—he says half the reason women need admitting for high blood-pressure in pregnancy is because they've had to wait hours in antenatal clinics—which reminds me, Melissa, you were coming to see me this afternoon. I'm going to have to cancel my clinic. I'm sorry.'

'Don't worry about it. I'll be seeing plenty of you in the next couple of days. When Amy picks up, I'll bring us a cup of tea and we'll have a chat about it here.'

They both looked at the little girl, her cheeks pale now except for two hectic spots of colour. She had fallen into a restless, fitful sleep, and Jo stroked her hair back from her forehead and sighed. 'She looks awful, doesn't she?' she said with a tremble in her voice, and Melissa put her arm round her shoulders and gave her a little hug.

'She'll be all right now, Jo. Give her time. Her heart's slowing a little, and her temperature hasn't gone up any more.'

'Should we sponge her down?'

Andrew came over to them and perched on the end

of the bed, regarding the little girl thoughtfully. 'It wouldn't hurt—use warm water, and just on her extremities. She's not in shock any more; the plasma's arrived—has she vomited again recently?'

Jo shook her head. 'Not since we brought her in.'

'Good. I think she's had enough stressful procedures without passing a nasogastric tube, but if she starts again we'll have to consider it. In the meantime we'll let her sleep.'

He turned to Josh. 'Are you on tonight? I'd like someone around and we're out.'

Josh nodded. 'Yes—I'm on call. I'll sleep at the hospital tonight.'

Andrew's brow creased. 'I thought you lived in.'

Melissa held her breath as Josh turned a slow smile on her.

'I've moved to Melissa's,' he said calmly.

Jo and Andrew both swivelled to look at her. She blushed furiously.

'In his parents' caravan. He's camping on my drive—he says I need a keeper.' Her voice was brittle, and, although she could see Jo dying to ask questions, both she and Andrew were mercifully silent.

Josh, on the other hand, shot her a cheeky grin, winked and walked away, leaving her floundering in the awkward silence. Andrew diplomatically followed him.

'Er—shall we sponge Amy?' she suggested wildly.

'What a good idea—and while we do that,' Jo replied, 'you can tell me why that gorgeous man is sleeping on your drive instead of in your bed.'

CHAPTER SEVEN

THE house seemed desperately lonely and empty that night. Melissa kept looking out at the caravan shrouded in darkness, and chastising herself for her stupidity.

How could she be so perverse? She didn't *want* him there, so how could she mind so much when he wasn't?

It was a ridiculous, untenable situation, and compounding it by spreading even more rumours round the hospital was just the giddy limit.

She hadn't had an opportunity to chastise him for that yet, but she would. Oh, yes. She was just itching for their next conversation!

Under normal circumstances Jo would have been trying to pump her for information all day, but her interest was definitely defused by worry over Amy, anyway, so Melissa felt she had probably escaped lightly.

Fortunately the little girl was showing signs of improvement, and, although the results had confirmed the meningococcal form of septicaemia, Josh had jumped on it so promptly that she had begun to respond almost immediately.

By the morning Melissa expected to see great signs of improvement—at which point, of course, Jo would then remember Josh's words and start to pump Melissa. She sighed.

Wretched man. He was getting her into so much trouble. If only he'd just quietly fade into the woodwork and let her get on with her life—but that wasn't Josh's way. He was stubborn, pig-headed and imagined he was in love with her.

It made him a determined opponent.

Well, he was no more determined than Melissa, and she had the great advantage of being boiling, hopping mad.

That, and the fact that she missed him, kept her awake most of the night.

The change in Amy in the fourteen hours since Melissa had last seen her was nothing short of a miracle. She was off the drip, her colour was normal, and although she still had a slight temperature and was very washed out she was obviously much better. The cannula was still in her arm just in case, but it seemed unlikely that she would need another infusion and Josh was justifiably pleased with her progress.

'Thank God for modern drugs,' he said in a quiet moment to Melissa. 'Forty years ago we would have lost her.'

'I wonder where she got it from?' Melissa pondered.

'Anywhere. We'll never know. It must have entered her system through the bite when she scratched it, but it's most unusual. Perhaps the bite was a red herring. The only relevant thing is her recovery, and that seems assured. Her bowel sounds returned during the night and she's kept down a few sips of water, so we decided to take the drip down.'

'But you've left the cannula in—do you anticipate trouble?' Melissa asked him, wondering if he had had another hunch.

He shook his head. 'No, I was just hedging my bets. She doesn't seem to mind having it in, and I didn't fancy trying to repeat the procedure in an emergency! Anyway, it's useful for bloods and drugs.'

A silence fell between them, and, meeting her eyes, Josh gave her a wary smile. 'I get the feeling I'm in trouble,' he murmured.

'Too damn right. Why did you have to say anything about where you're living?'

He shrugged. 'It can't really be a secret. People talk endlessly—their lives are so drab and dull they need gossip to enliven them——'

'So you chucked me to the lions to stop them getting bored! Well, thanks a bunch——'

'Hardly the lions,' he protested gently. 'Andrew knows all about us now, and Jo's a friend of yours anyway.'

She snorted. 'It was Jo who told me I ought to get on with it if I wanted a baby. I think she's now suffering a massive fit of conscience.'

'Why massive?' he said in surprise. 'You've got what you wanted——'

'Have I?' she asked softly. 'Actually I think I got a heck of a lot more than I bargained for.'

His mouth twisted in wry acknowledgement. 'Why do I get the feeling you don't think that's a plus?'

She snorted. 'I wanted peace and quiet, a child of my own to love and raise without interference or any strings attached, no possibility of anyone getting hurt, and what did I get? You.'

She made it sound like a dirty word, and had an instant surge of remorse at the flash of pain on his face.

She could see him withdraw from her, gathering himself in and retreating into his shell, and she wished she could unsay the words. No, not the words, but the tone of them, the hurtful denigration of all his good qualities.

It wasn't Josh's fault their relationship wouldn't work.

Sudden, weary tears filled her eyes and she turned away.

'I'm sorry. I didn't mean it to come out like that.'

There was silence for a moment, then she heard him give a tired and impatient sigh.

'Yes, you did,' he said quietly. 'The trouble is that babies, by definition, have strings attached, and the string holding me to mine has the strength of a steel hawser. I know you don't like it, but it's the truth. I'm sorry if I don't conform to your expectations of a docile sperm donor, but you could always have avoided the problem by coming clean at the beginning and asking me what my attitude would be.'

There was a discreet cough behind them, and Melissa closed her eyes and sighed.

'Yes, Anna?'

'Could you do the premeds with me, please? There isn't another qualified member of staff on.'

She took a steadying breath and turned. Josh was standing in the doorway of her office and she had to squeeze by him to get out.

As she did so the baby wriggled, and their eyes locked, hers anguished, his filled with an emotion she didn't dare to define.

'Damn you, Lissa,' he said softly. 'I won't give up, you know. It's mine, and I intend to make sure it knows that, right from the start. You won't get rid of me.'

Somehow that didn't surprise her one little bit.

He was going to fight for the baby. She knew it in her bones, with every cell of her body. He was biding his time, but in due course, when it was born, he was going to fight her for it.

She fretted about it all that day and through the following night, then in the afternoon while Jo was watching Amy sleep Melissa made two cups of tea and went and sat in the little room with them.

'I've brought you a cuppa,' she told Jo.

'Oh, saint. I've been dying for one but she's been

so demanding. I think she's better.' Jo eyed Melissa thoughtfully, and tutted. 'You look shattered. I don't think you should still be working full-time.'

Melissa shook her head and gave a little laugh. 'It's not the work.'

'Josh?'

She took a deep breath, then said in a rush, 'I think he's going to go for custody. He said he intended to make sure the baby knew from the start it was his—that I wouldn't get rid of him. I'm sure he's going to go to court for joint custody, at the very least.'

Jo chewed her lip worriedly. 'God, I feel so responsible for this mess. When I said if you wanted a child you ought to get on with it in the near future, I never for a moment thought you'd do anything so precipitate as rush out and grab the first decent man you saw!'

Melissa blushed. 'It wasn't really like that. I didn't want to trap some poor unwary man into a marriage I didn't want just to have a baby, and anyway there was always the possibility I couldn't conceive. Imagine, marrying a man just to get a child from him and then not being able to get pregnant! I'd be stuck with two impossible situations!'

'You could always adopt,' Jo said quietly.

'Oh, Jo—it wouldn't be the same. It was different for you and Alex, you loved each other anyway. Not being able to have children was really a bit of a red herring——'

Jo's bitter little laugh cut her off. 'You think so? I nearly didn't marry him because of it. I couldn't believe he would want me just for myself. I was so worried he was marrying me just because it was his baby that caused me to haemorrhage and have the hysterectomy. I was convinced he was only marrying me out of guilt.'

'Josh wants to marry me,' Melissa told her. 'I think that's guilt, too, and also because it's the easiest way to have his child. The trouble is, I know it won't last.'

Jo looked surprised. 'Whyever not?'

Melissa waved her hands expansively. 'You only have to look at him! He's too gorgeous for his own good, and how on earth am I going to be able to hold him? I've already got one little stretch mark. By the time I've finished I'll have millions, and a saggy stomach and droopy boobs and anyway, I'm older than him——'

'What on earth's that got to do with the price of fish? Age is immaterial. If he was older than you, you wouldn't turn a hair.'

'It isn't me who'll be going off with someone younger,' she said drily. 'And besides,' she added in a flat, matter-of-fact voice that disguised her fears, 'I might need a hysterectomy anyway, so no more children.'

Jo eyed her thoughtfully. 'How have you been?'

She shrugged. 'OK. I get the occasional pain for a few days, then it sharpens, like a little rip inside, and then it's better after that. I think it might be old lesions separating as the baby grows.'

Jo nodded. 'Very possibly. How about the old symptoms?'

She shook her head. 'No, none.'

'I don't suppose you know whether it hurts to make love—that would be a good indicator of the progress of your disease.'

She blushed. 'It doesn't,' she mumbled.

Jo gave her an odd look. 'Melissa, I don't want to interfere, but if you're still that close——'

'We're not!'

'You're not?'

'It was a one-off—an accident. A moment of weakness. It won't happen again.'

'Pity.' Jo grinned at her. 'It seems a shame to waste

him, when he's so clearly besotted with you.'

Melissa stared at her. 'He's not besotted.'

Jo just arched a slender brow and said nothing.

'He's not,' Melissa said again, more quietly. 'He thinks he loves me, but I know it's just because of the baby.'

'So why did he follow you up here?'

Melissa shrugged. 'Search me. Because he hadn't finished with me? Men like to be the one to walk away— their egos cope better with it that way round. Anyway, physically it was——' She blushed and broke off. 'Perhaps he just felt we had unfinished business.'

'And perhaps you still have, and always will have.'

Melissa stood up. 'No chance. The only thing we have in common is the baby, and it's mine! He's not having it, if I have to go through every court in the land to keep him away!'

She spun on her heel and walked straight into Josh's chest. With a little cry she pushed past him, ran through the ward and shot into her office, closing the door behind her.

A minute later it opened and Josh came in. 'Lissa?' he murmured.

'Go away.'

'No. You can't go round flinging down the gauntlet like that and then refusing to let me pick it up! What was that all about?'

She stood with her back to him for a second, then spun round, eyes blazing. 'You! You think you can cajole and sweet-talk me and take me to bed and wind me round your little finger, and then when that fails you coerce and bully and threaten me and talk about taking my baby away——'

She broke off, tears streaming down her face, and after a second of astonished silence Josh put his arms round her and smoothed her hair.

'Hush, now, silly girl—I never talked about taking your baby away——!'

'You did!' She pushed him away and straightened up, scrubbing the tears from her cheeks and glaring up at him. 'You said you wouldn't give up! You said it was your baby, and you were going to make sure it knew that right from the start——'

'I am. That doesn't mean you aren't allowed to be its mother. I have never intended to take the baby from you and I wouldn't. I think that's a terrible thing to do, from everybody's point of view. What I want is harmonious access to my child, preferably on a daily basis because we're living together, married, just like any other conventional parents. Why is that so difficult for you to understand?'

'Because I can't trust you,' she cried. 'How do I know when you're lying?'

He regarded her steadily for a moment. 'You don't. You just have to take my word for it, and that's something you'll have to come to terms with. Maybe time will prove to you that I don't want to hurt you. In the meantime, I think we can send Amy Carter home now. Would you like to sort out her antibiotics while I do the letter?'

And with that he turned on his heel and left her.

Things were strained between them after that. They communicated at work whenever necessary, and at home she did her best to ignore his presence, closing her curtains whenever she was in the sitting-room so she didn't have to put up with the unsettling sensation of his watching her all the time.

Not that he did. He probably never even glanced up at her, she thought with a sniff of disdain. Nor would she want him to, but she was suffering a perverse lack of good judgement over him at the moment.

It must be her hormones, or maybe it was the quietly reproachful look in those beautiful blue eyes, the look that said, 'Trust me. Would I lie to you?'

Probably.

She found the work more and more demanding, and then, when she finally got to see Jo at the antenatal clinic, her blood-pressure was creeping up.

'You've got to cut down your work or give up,' Jo told her firmly. 'Everything else looks very good, and I'm extremely pleased with the way your disease has stayed in remission. I think you may well have beaten it, but you'll only know after the baby's born—you will breast-feed, won't you, to keep the hormones going as long as possible?'

'Yes, of course. I intended to anyway.'

'So, about work.'

Melissa sighed. 'I've only got another three weeks——'

'That's too long. I want you on part-time this week, and if that improves the situation you can continue on part-time for the next two weeks. If it doesn't, you're going to have to stop.'

Melissa chewed her lip. 'They haven't got my relief until the middle of October. If I give up now they'll be in real difficulties.'

'Then you have to do the bare essentials at work, delegate whenever possible and take the quiet jobs instead of the very active ones. You forget, I saw you at work. You're constantly on the go, and it has to stop. Do as little as possible at home, rest whenever you can and come and see me again next Monday.'

'Yes, sir,' Melissa said with a rueful smile.

Jo grinned. 'That's the attitude. By the way, Amy sends her love.'

'How is she?'

'Fine. Fit as a flea. I still can't get over how fast she

went down and how quickly she came back up, thanks to Josh. He was wonderful.'

'He is,' Melissa said softly, a little bubble of pride inside her. Jo gave her a funny look, and she added swiftly, 'A wonderful doctor.'

Jo's smile was knowing. 'Of course,' she said soothingly. 'Now, remember, rest, cut down, and come and see me next week.'

'Will do. Thanks.'

She went back to the ward, fiddled with the rota to engineer some time off, and delegated the others to cover the more physical parts of the job.

'I'll sit at the computer and do the specialling and cuddle the babies—you lot can deal with young Simon and his ilk,' she told her staff.

'Wow, thanks,' Anna said drily.

She thought she would hate the enforced idleness, but curiously she found a great deal of pleasure in the backwaters of her ward. She was around for decision-making and procedures that necessitated her input, but for the most part she involved herself in coaxing unhappy and sore children to eat, or sleep, or just relax.

She found time to read to children, and often would look up to find several had gathered round.

On one occasion she even found Josh on the periphery, a strange look on his face. When she looked up he gave her a sheepish smile and faded away, leaving her with a curious, unsettled feeling inside.

One evening towards the end of that week he knocked on her kitchen door. She was just considering making supper when she heard his footsteps approaching, then the light rap.

Opening the door, she looked up at him, not sure what he would want, and was amazed when he invited her to join him in the caravan for a meal.

Whatever she had expected, it wasn't that.

'Um—I don't—I was just about to——'

'It's ready now—I just have to stir the crème fraîche into the sauce. Please?'

Crème fraîche? 'What sauce?' she asked, weakening.

'For the beef stroganoff.'

Her mouth watered instantly. 'Um—can I bring anything?'

He smiled. 'Just yourself.'

She shouldn't have come, she thought later as she tucked her feet up and settled herself comfortably in the corner of one of the seating units. It really was quite a pleasant caravan inside, really very warm and cosy, and not nearly as tacky as she'd imagined.

That was the trouble, of course. It was all too easy to sit there, sipping a glass of superbly smooth Zinfandel and chatting to Josh, but he was sneaking under her guard again and one carefully chosen word and she would fall into bed with him again.

And therein lay the cause of her downfall. She still found him devastatingly attractive, and knowing and liking the man himself just made walking away even harder.

The fact that he was a man and therefore by definition she couldn't trust him was neither here nor there. Her hormones just weren't interested in rational argument——

'What?'

'I said, your eyes are drooping and it's time you went to bed. Jo wants you to rest.'

Her brows gathered together in a little pucker. 'Jo?'

'Carter—your gynaecologist. She wants you to rest, do nothing and take care. I'm just obeying her orders. I've fed you, made you sit down, and now I'm sending you to bed.'

And Melissa had thought it was a spontaneous gesture! What a mug.

She went, remembering to thank him politely for a delicious dinner, and cried herself to sleep.

The following day she avoided him, and that evening she shut her curtains as soon as she arrived home. When the knock came on the door she told him she was in the bath.

'In the dark?' he said. 'Come on, Melissa, open the door.'

She opened it, a belligerent expression on her face, and he held out a covered plate.

'I have to go back to the hospital, I'm on duty and Rob's called me to say they've had a child in with crush injuries. I have to go back now and I'll probably stay there all night. I just wanted to be sure you were all right.'

She took the plate, thanked him rather distractedly and watched him go, then thoughtfully closed the door.

Did he have to be so considerate?

The plate was cold. She took the bowl off the top and found a portion of fresh salmon, some rice salad and slivers of fresh avocado and melon nestled in frilly lettuce. Ravenous, she ate it in seconds and washed it down with a cup of tea, pondering on his motives.

Care of his child?

He was taking it to extremes, if so. Perhaps Jo had put the frighteners on him—maybe her blood-pressure hike was more significant than she had realised?

Deep in thought, she made another cup of tea, switched off the television and went to bed with a book.

She read about two lines before sleep claimed her.

The child with crush injuries was in a bad way still when she arrived at work the following morning. She was only five, a tiny little mite for her age, and there was no sign of her mother.

'She had to go home last night to the others—said

she'd come back in the morning,' Josh told her. 'It probably hasn't mattered—the kid's been out of it most of the time. Her name's Boo, apparently.'

'Boo?'

He shrugged. 'The mother wasn't very forthcoming, I gather. She'd already left by the time I got here.'

Melissa smoothed back the child's damp, straggly hair and felt her heart reach out to the little scrap. 'How did it happen? Do we know?'

He shook his head. 'The mother apparently found her in the car park outside her block of flats. She must have been hit or squashed against a wall by a car, judging by the nature of her injuries. From the gravel in her knees we think she was kneeling when she was hit—possibly trying to avoid the collision. The police were here for hours. They wanted to talk to the mother but she had to go. One of them took her home, and another stayed here. They were hoping Boo would wake up, I think.'

'And did she?'

Josh shook his head. 'No chance. We gave her some fairly hefty pain relief and she just went out like a light, thank God.' He paused for a moment. 'She was terrified. If you look at her you'll see evidence of cigarette burns and other old and definitely not accidental injuries. No, someone's been gunning for this kid for some considerable time, and I just hope they don't win this time.'

'Is it likely?' Melissa looked at the tiny child on the bed, her body wired up to a monitor, tubes in and out of her in all possible places, and shook her head. 'We can't let her die, Josh.'

'I don't intend to, but there's a limit to how well we can play God. She's fairly stable now, but she needs watching like a hawk. That chest, particularly, worries me.'

'I'll special her,' Melissa said, and after sorting out the jobs that couldn't be delegated, she relieved the nurse by Boo's side and settled down to watch her and record her blood-pressure, pulse and respirations every fifteen minutes.

In between she read the case-notes. Crush injuries to the chest with three fractured ribs and a cracked breastbone, a lung that might be leaking air into the chest, fractures of both arms and one of the fingers on her left hand, and then internal abdominal injuries which seemed fortunately limited to bruising of the left kidney, spleen and liver. Nothing seemed to have ruptured or been displaced, and her observations seemed fairly stable, although her respirations were a little erratic, Melissa noted.

She would watch them.

She had just completed the second lot of observations when a policeman came on to the ward and was brought over to her.

'Sister Shaw? I'm PC Burton.'

She looked at him and smiled. 'Hi. The last time I saw you you were arresting a goat in my front garden— after mistakenly arresting Dr Lancaster.'

He chuckled slightly. 'I remember it well, madam. The goat ate the corner of my jacket while I was walking her home.' His smile faded, and he jerked his head at the child on the bed. 'How is she?'

'Not good.'

He nodded thoughtfully. 'Had to come and tell you—mother's done a bunk. The neighbours say she packed her stuff up and went, about three this morning, after we left her. Took the other kids and went. We arrested a man round there this morning, drunk as a skunk and demanding to know where we'd hidden her. The neighbours seem to think he might know something about how this young lady got her injuries.'

Melissa's eyes closed. 'Her father?' she asked, dreading the answer.

'Unlikely, madam,' the policeman said drily. 'We understand he'd been there off and on for a few months—apparently they were always fighting. She chucked him out last week. Looks like she's done a bunk to get rid of him, but not before he damaged the little one.'

Melissa looked at the tiny, fragile little girl lying bruised and battered under the sheet, a tube into her stomach to empty the contents in case of bowel complications, her arms in plaster, her chest a mass of contusions, a catheter to drain her urine and check on the blood lost by her damaged kidney, another tube into her leg to replace lost fluids—it made her want to scream in rage.

'How could anyone do such a wicked, wicked thing?' she asked furiously. 'To deliberately set out to hurt an innocent child—oh, it makes me so angry!'

She broke off, struggling with her temper, and then shook her head. 'I'm sorry. I just find it very difficult to deal with people who do that sort of thing.'

'You and me, both, madam. Now, when do you suppose this young lady will be able to talk to us?'

She shrugged. 'I have no idea. She's heavily sedated because of her injuries, and she'll be in a lot of pain when she starts to wake up—it could be days. At least another twenty-four hours, I'd say. Do you want us to contact you?'

'I think in view of the nature of her injuries we'll arrange for a member of the force to be here at all times until we've spoken to her and confirmed the neighbours' suspicions. In the meantime, we'll have to hope she continues to make good progress so we don't end up dealing with a murder enquiry.'

CHAPTER EIGHT

THE words sent a chill down Melissa's spine. All that day she sat with Boo, and all the next, waiting patiently for some improvement.

There was none, and her respirations continued to be erratic. Then they grew faster and more shallow, so they X-rayed her chest and found a shadow which might have been air or might have been blood, and continued to watch her closely.

Josh didn't want to do anything invasive like putting in a drain, and gradually her respirations seemed to settle and become more regular and a little slower. Again they settled back to wait. Often air in the chest cavity outside the lungs would resolve itself, and Melissa went off duty, still concerned but beginning to feel some hope.

Josh was on duty and didn't come back that night. Again she felt the loneliness his absence seemed to trigger without fail, and after moping about and wondering how Boo was she finally went to bed.

She didn't sleep very well, and she was just considering getting up to make a cup of tea when she heard Josh's car returning.

It was shortly before six, and she decided to get up, make the tea and then have a lazy bath before going to work.

She went down to the kitchen, turning on lights as she went, and as she plugged in the kettle there was a tap at the door.

'Melissa? It's me—can I come in?'

He sounded weary, and instantly she worried about

Boo. Although if she was worse he wouldn't be here——

She opened the door, and one look at his face told her the answer.

'Boo?' she said quietly, and he nodded.

'She died about an hour ago. She had a massive haemorrhage—we rushed her to Theatre and Gavin Jones opened her chest but he couldn't save her. There just wasn't enough warning. By the time he'd got her chest opened she'd gone.'

Melissa closed the door behind him, automatically got two mugs down and made the tea, her mind running over and over the case.

'She seemed better,' she said finally.

'Mmm. The lull before the storm. She started to come round a little, and coughed violently. That was it. There was apparently a blood vessel with a long graze on the wall, and the cough produced sufficient change in pressure to rupture the weakness. It was all over in minutes.'

He went on, 'The police were there at the time. They're off to charge the man with murder—apparently they found his car with dents on the bonnet and bumper that had fibres from her clothes pressed into them, and they also found tyre tracks in the vicinity that matched his. He hasn't confessed—it seems likely he doesn't remember because he was too drunk. He can't account for his movements at all that evening.'

'I hope the police make it stick,' she said flatly. 'Poor little girl. . . Has anyone tried to contact the mother?'

'The police are going to put an appeal in the Press for her to come forward. They need more evidence to charge him with earlier abuse, not only of Boo but the other children, and it seems likely he'll go down for a good long while.'

Melissa handed him a mug and led him through

into the sitting-room. She perched on the edge of the settee, staring blindly across the room. She couldn't see or think about anything except that little tiny girl, and it was very difficult to keep her professional detachment.

A tear trickled down her cheek and she scrubbed it away absently. 'I should be used to this sort of thing by now,' she said, her voice unsteady.

'Murder? I hope not.'

She looked up and met Josh's eyes, and they were every bit as sad as hers. She leant against him and accepted the warmth of his embrace. The silent comfort seemed to ease the tight, desolate feeling inside, and after a few minutes she sat up away from him and sipped at her tea.

They talked about Boo for a few more minutes, and about child abuse and violence and what could be done to prevent it.

'It's indicative of a lack of respect in the whole of society,' Josh said heavily. 'Nobody cares about anyone or anything except themselves any more. Consideration seems to be a thing of the past.'

Melissa thought of the consideration he had shown her, bringing her meals, cooking for her, living in a cold caravan to protect her—even coming over this morning to tell her about Boo had been an act of consideration.

'Thank you for telling me about her before I got on the ward,' she said quietly.

'It's OK. I saw the lights on and I knew you'd want a minute to get used to the idea before you got to work.' He picked up a little pair of dungarees she'd been finishing the night before, and smiled gently at her. 'Hedging your bets?'

They were pink and blue striped, and she had to smile. 'I should have gone for green and yellow, but

I didn't want the baby to look like a jaundiced cater-
pillar.'

Josh chuckled. 'Poor little beast. It has no idea
what's in store for it. I'm going to have to monitor
the colour scheming, I think, or he'll grow up with a
gender crisis.'

'Rubbish,' she dismissed. 'It's a girl, and anyway
I've seen you in a pink shirt.'

'Raspberry,' he corrected. 'And I'm quite aware of
my gender, thank you.'

Melissa looked away. So, unfortunately, was she.

'While we're actually talking, my mother asked if
you'd join us for Christmas. The whole family usually
descends—it's quite fun.'

She felt overwhelmed at the thought of his entire
family, all gathered together in the same place and
dying of curiosity.

'I might have had the baby by then,' she improvised
while she flailed around her another excuse.

'Of course—but you might not.'

She forced herself to meet his eyes. 'What do you
want me to do?'

'Me?' He smiled wryly. 'I'd like you to come,
but, if you really feel you can't face them all, just
say so.'

She chewed her lip. 'Could I leave my options
open?'

He chuckled. 'Now, how did I know you'd say that?
Yes, of course you can leave your options open. One
more won't make any difference either way.' He
checked his watch and stood up. 'I'd better go and get
ready for work, I suppose.'

She went with him to the door.

'Thanks for telling me about Boo,' she said as he
opened it.

He turned and hugged her gently. 'You're welcome.

You'd better hurry—I've held you up. I'll see you at the hospital.'

There was a hush on the ward when she went in, the sort of hush that only tragedy could create.

The bustle was there, of course, because the ward was busy and it was an operating day, but underlying it all the staff and children were subdued.

Even young Simon was quiet. He was scheduled for more surgery on his left leg, the one which had been most badly shattered and was showing a great reluctance to heal. Nick Davidson was going to repin and replate the ankle and would try to rebuild his heel, and he was going down to Theatre that afternoon.

Maybe it was that, or maybe it was Boo's death that made him so quiet. Whatever, instead of being reassured Melissa was worried about him. She found time in the midst of the chaotic morning to go and sit with him.

'Do you want to talk about your operation?' she asked after a moment.

He shrugged nonchalantly.

'Are you worried about how you'll feel afterwards?'

Again he shrugged. 'It'll hurt, I know that. It always does.'

'Is your mum coming up later?'

'Maybe.'

'She usually does when you have an op, doesn't she?'

'She's at work today. I don't expect she can make it. Anyway, it looks sissy having my mum here.'

Melissa laughed softly. 'Rubbish. It's all very well being tough, but there are times when we all need support from the people who love us.'

He gave her a curious look. 'Can I ask you something?'

She should have been warned, but she wasn't.

'Of course,' she replied calmly. 'What is it?'

'Are you going to marry Dr Lancaster?'

She stared at him in blank surprise, then hot colour flooded her cheeks. 'Really, Simon, I don't think that's any of your business,' she managed at last.

'Sorry. It's just that we know the baby's his and you aren't married any more, and we just wondered—well, he's a really great guy and we thought it would be really cool if you got together and stuff. . .'

And stuff. Why did kids end every sentence with 'and stuff'? she wondered abstractedly while most of her mind dealt with the knotty problem of all the children in the ward discussing her marital status and the paternity of her baby!

'My dad didn't care about my mum,' Simon went on. 'He did a bunk when I was three weeks old, and we haven't seen him since.' His mouth twisted in a tragic little smile. 'I would've liked a dad—someone to play football with and stuff. Still, me and Mum cope OK without him, so I don't suppose it matters. Bit hard on her, though, having to earn enough to keep us. She was only sixteen, she hadn't done much at school——'

He gave an expressive little shrug. 'She has to take work when she's offered it. That's why she can't come in today, 'cos she daren't have time off. Her boss got a bit stroppy and said if it happened again she'd have to go.'

'What a shame. Still, I'm sure she'll be thinking about you and she'll be in this evening, won't she?'

'Yeah—I'll see her then. About that kid——?'

'Boo?'

'Yeah. She died, right?'

Melissa watched him closely. 'Yes, she did.'

'While she was having an operation.'

So that was it.

'No, she died before they could complete the operation that might have saved her. They weren't quick enough, unfortunately. It just all happened too fast. She didn't die *because* of the operation.'

'Oh.' He was quiet for a second, then fiddled with the edge of the sheet. 'But people do die in operations, don't they?'

There was no alternative to honesty. 'Yes, they do. Sometimes they have an allergic reaction to the anaesthetic, but almost always they are people who haven't had an anaesthetic before, or not for a long time. You've had tons, and we know you're fine with them. You don't even get sick like most kids. Otherwise they are people like Boo who are very, very seriously ill indeed and certainly wouldn't live without the operation.'

He was thoughtful still. 'What about blood clots?'

Education was a curse, she thought. 'Yes, sometimes people get blood clots from operations and they can cause complications that occasionally prove fatal. It's quite rare, though, and usually easily treatable.'

'So,' he said, finally winding up to the punch-line, 'what are the odds?'

'Of your coming back here to give us strain for another few weeks? I should think intolerably high.'

He regarded her steadily for a moment, then a smile crept on to his face. 'Thanks.'

Risking his pride, she leant forwards and hugged him. 'You're welcome, you little rascal. Now, how about a game? Can I get one of the others to bring something over so you can play?'

'Yeah—hey, Lucien, bring that red box over. . .no, the bottom one. That's it. Let's have a game.'

She left him looking a little happier, and went back to her pre-ops. Josh appeared at her side. 'What was all that about?'

'He was worried about dying under the anaesthetic. I think I managed to reassure him. Oh, and he also wants to know if we're getting married as I'm having your baby.'

Josh gave a short, surprised laugh. 'Did he, by Jove? And are we?'

She gave him a repressive glare. 'No, we are not.'

He nodded, his face set in mock resignation. 'Just checking,' he said, and his lips lifted in a lop-sided, wry grin. 'Keep me posted if there's any change.'

'There won't be.'

'Never say die,' he murmured under his breath, and then he went off down the corridor, whistling softly.

Simon's operation went well later that day, and he was returned to them shortly before Melissa went off duty, still very drowsy but obviously alive.

'I said we'd get you back,' she told him fondly, and he gave her a weak grin before his eyelids drooped and he went back to sleep.

It was the weekend, and Melissa was looking forward to putting her feet up and doing nothing.

Josh, however, had no such intentions. She was in the bath on Saturday morning just before twelve when she heard a scraping, bumping noise on the front wall of her cottage.

She leapt out of the bath in time to see Josh climbing up a ladder right by the bathroom window.

She grabbed a towel, wrapped it round herself and flung the window open. 'You pervert!' she shrieked. 'What are you doing spying on me in the bath?'

'I wasn't——' he began, but then the ladder started to slide, he made a grab for the guttering and with a grinding creak it detached itself from the eaves and swung out across the garden, depositing Josh in the apple tree.

He gave a startled yelp as the branch gave way, and there was an awful ripping sound as he dropped to the grass, his shirt and pride in tatters.

Getting to his feet, he glowered up at her framed in the bathroom window, dripping wet and clad only in a towel. She started to giggle, and he planted his hands on his hips and glared at her.

'What's so damn funny?' he growled.

'You are. What were you doing anyway, climbing that ladder outside the bathroom window?'

'Putting you up an outside light,' he snarled. 'So much for your maidenly gratitude!'

'Huh!' She tossed her hair back. 'As you very well know, I'm not a maiden, and anyway you should have asked. Maybe I didn't want an outside light?'

'Lady, you need an outside light. How are you going to manage getting back home in the winter and having to wrestle all the baby equipment through the apple tree in the dark?'

Damn. He was being considerate again.

'Well, that branch certainly won't be in the way any more,' she said with the last vestige of her humour. 'And now you've got to mend the guttering as well. Still,' she peered into it, 'it needed emptying. You could do that while it's hanging there—make it easier to get the bits out.'

He shot her one last, baleful look and turned to pick up the ladder. As he did so she saw the blood that was seeping into his torn shirt.

'Josh, you're hurt!' she cried.

'Tell me about it,' he grumbled. 'I had noticed.'

She shut the window, dried herself briskly and tugged on her robe before running downstairs.

She yanked open the door. 'Come here, let me look at that.'

He stopped what he was doing and eyed her cynically. 'Dare I trust you?'

'It's a case of having to. You can't reach or see to do it yourself.'

He put the tools down and came cautiously towards her. 'It's damn sore—don't you go splashing antiseptic into it with gay abandon.'

'Would I?' she said soothingly, turning him round. 'You'll have to take your shirt off.'

He sighed shortly and peeled off his shirt, revealing a warm, solid expanse of satin skin with a six-inch gouge through the middle of it.

'Ouch,' she said softly. 'I'll wash it; it's got bits of tree in.'

'I knew it,' he muttered. 'She's going to torture me, Calico. Why do you stick it?'

The cat miaowed in commiseration. 'You see? Even the cat agrees.'

'Rubbish. The cat's hungry as usual. Come on, in the sitting-room. I want you at the table, leaning over so I can get at it.'

'Oh, Granny, what a big bottle of antiseptic,' he sing-songed. 'All the better to torture you with, my dear.'

'Shut up, Little Red Riding Hood,' she ordered. 'You're a full-grown man. You should be able to cope with a little bit of antiseptic.'

He made a rude noise but sat obediently with his arms folded on the table and his head laid on them. 'All right?'

She eyed the smooth skin stretched taut over firm, well-honed muscles and swallowed. 'You'll do. OK, I'm going to swab it now.'

He swore softly under his breath, but to his credit he didn't move a muscle.

'OK? she asked.

'What do you think?'

'I think you'll live. I'll cover it. Now, about this light——'

'It's a passive infra-red detector light, it will come on automatically when anyone approaches it, and it will give you security and make getting in and out easier and safer for you. All right? Now, where would you like me to put it?'

She bit her lip, and he twisted round and tutted at her. 'Lady, you have a deplorable sense of humour. Where *on the wall*?'

'Over the door?'

'That's what I thought. Now, if I could have a little positive input perhaps I'll survive the exercise.'

He stood up, cobbled his torn shirt into one hand and went back out to his caravan, emerging a moment later in a clean shirt.

The light was finished by two, at which point her conscience got the better of her and she made him lunch. Then he cleaned out and repaired the gutter, emptied the other gutter at the back and then washed both cars. It was headily domestic, and she caught herself happily humming as she ironed her uniform dress ready for Monday.

It stopped her in her tracks. What was she doing, playing house with him like this?

He came in. 'All done,' he said with a grin. 'Do I get a reward?'

'No. It's a pity you stopped short of doing the caravan.'

He blinked a little at her tone, but without a word he filled the bucket again and went back out. An hour later she was racked with guilt but the caravan was sparkling and looked much less foul.

He came back with a grin. 'Better?'

'Much.'

'Good. What would you like me to do now—furniture polish on the inside of the drains?'

She grinned sheepishly. 'Am I being foul?'

'Just a bit.' He put the bucket down and looked at her. 'Can I make us both a cup of tea, or is that presuming?'

She felt ashamed of her pettiness. 'Tea would be lovely,' she said.

To her surprise he went back to the caravan, emerging a while later to call her.

She turned off the iron—she was bored with it anyway—and went across to his caravan, noting in passing how much easier it was to get past the apple tree since he had landed in it.

There was a huge golden-brown fruit cake in the middle of the table, stuffed with juicy raisins and cherries, and he waved the knife at it. 'Mum made it—want a bit?'

She had two, and then sat back with a groan. 'Oh, I'm a pig. There isn't room in there any more for such greed.'

'You need food—you're looking skinnier.'

'Skinnier?' she laughed like a drain. 'You must be joking! I'm like a house—God knows what it'll be like by Christmas.'

He looked steadily at her, his eyes concerned. 'Your face is thinner. You look strained. Is that me?'

She was silenced for a minute, then shook her head. 'No, it's not you, I'm tired. I'm not sleeping too well.'

'How much longer have you got at work?' he asked.

'Two weeks.'

He nodded. 'You could do with some fresh air. Why don't we go for a walk tomorrow in the woods? We could go and borrow Bella from my parents—she hardly ever gets taken out for a run any more since most of us left home. She'd love it.'

Her mouth, running on autopilot, agreed to go while her mind was still deciding it was a silly thing to do, and so the following morning they set off in his car at ten-thirty, picked up Bella from a lovely red-brick Georgian farmhouse near Orford on the coast and went for a walk through the forest at Tunstall.

A group of riders passed them and waved cheerily, and Melissa sat on a fallen log and watched as Josh threw sticks for Bella.

Poor old girl, she was getting a bit ancient to chase sticks for long, but she still came back with a happy wag and dropped them expectantly at Josh's feet.

When she had had a little rest they set off again, and Melissa had an overpowering urge to hold his hand and lean against him. Instead she stuffed her hands in her pockets to keep them out of the way and made bright and inconsequential little remarks.

It occurred to her later that Josh was very quiet during their walk, but maybe he just didn't feel like talking. He was a garrulous person.

They arrived back at his parents' house, and before she got out of the car, he laid a hand on her arm. 'Mum's going to ask us to stay for lunch. There's no one else here today—Matthew's gone to a friend and the others aren't here. I'm just warning you so you've got time to think up an excuse if you don't want to stay.'

She was surprised to find she did want to, but no more surprised than Josh. He looked almost stunned, and then a smile softened his features and he winked at her. Heavens, did it really mean so much to him that they should stay?

She didn't regret her decision. The meal was wonderful, his parents were incredibly easy to get on with and she was so relaxed that she even fell asleep after lunch, curled up on a chair in the sunny end of the drawing-room while the others chatted quietly over coffee.

When she woke she was embarrassed, but Mrs Lancaster tutted at her.

'You need your sleep for the baby—you're looking exhausted. You should rest.'

Her husband gave a snort. 'You never did.'

'Fat chance with so many of them under foot. This is the only chance you'll have where you can really take it easy, and you ought to. Once it comes along your life will never be the same again.'

Melissa looked at Josh, and a heavy sadness settled over her. It wouldn't; Mrs Lancaster was right. Once her baby was born the focus of Josh's concern and tenderness would transfer from her to the baby, and she would lose him, bit by bit.

It was a terrifying thought.

CHAPTER NINE

On Monday morning Melissa went into work to find Simon looking thoroughly fed up but very much alive.

'How're you doing, sport?' she asked him with a grin.

'It hurts,' he grumbled. 'It was just getting better, and it's all messed up again.'

'But it wasn't getting better, was it? That was the whole point. Now, you will be careful and stay off it this time to give it a chance to heal, won't you?'

He snorted rudely. 'If it hurts like this there's no way I'm walking anywhere, mate!' His face fell, and he sighed. 'Sometimes I think I won't ever be able to get out of this bed.'

'You can have a wheelchair and move yourself around in it once the pain wears off and the danger of swelling has passed—but only if you promise not to be a pain and don't zoom round the place like a Formula One driver, knocking everybody over!'

'Oh, spoilsport,' he said with a grin, and she knuckled his chin and left him to have a rest.

He did doze a little, which was a measure of how rotten he felt, and when Nick Davidson came round she asked for stronger pain relief for him.

'He'll walk on it,' Nick warned.

'Not if you threaten him with another op.'

Nick grunted, clearly unconvinced, but wrote him up for some more pethidine. 'Just for the next twenty-four hours. After that he'll have to have paracetamol and dihydrocodeine.'

'Then he'll get constipated and die of embarrassment

if we have to give him an enema again.'

'So give him Lactulose and senna and lots of fibre—and make him take it. The remembered embarrassment should help,' Nick grinned and went to check his other patients, and Melissa found herself with time to read to some of the little ones.

It was getting difficult to cuddle children on her lap, so she ended up sitting on the playroom floor on a beanbag with a cluster of children round her, sprawled against her in a heap.

Josh found her like that and grinned. 'You remind me of Bella when she had her puppies,' he said, and there was a tenderness in his tone that brought a lump to her throat.

Oh, damn the man. . .

She went and saw Jo after she finished work, because the antenatal clinic ran into the evening to give workers a chance to attend. Jo was pleased with her, said her blood-pressure had come down a little and she looked less awful.

'Are you getting any exercise?' Jo asked.

'Oh, yes—we went for a walk yesterday.'

'We?'

Blast. Trust Jo to pick it up. 'Josh thought his parents' dog deserved a run, so we went over to the coast and walked through the forest, then had lunch with his parents, which probably undid all the good of the walk.'

'I doubt it,' Jo said drily, but she was clearly fascinated that Melissa was spending so much time with Josh.

'So, ah, things are looking up, are they?' she fished.

Melissa, however, refused to be drawn on the subject, denying that they were getting closer together.

'I'm not going to marry him, Jo,' she said emphatically. 'It's not an option.'

Jo said nothing, instead changing the subject and booking Melissa's next appointment.

'Are you going to come to the childbirth classes here?' she asked.

'I expect so. Do I need to book?'

'Yes, but that's not a problem. They're every Tuesday. The receptionist will give you details. The next class starts in a fortnight, so that will fit in perfectly with finishing at work.'

Melissa was dreading the thought of all that time on her hands. The baby's room needed decorating, but otherwise she was ready to go. Her case was packed, the little clothes were bought or made and lined up in a chest of drawers, nappies and bedding and a cot and carry-cot were all waiting to be delivered. The time was going to drag endlessly, she was sure.

She drove home, wondering if Josh would be back or not, cross with herself for even thinking about it.

He was back, and he was listening to what sounded like a golden oldies compilation rock album. It was foot-tapping, hum-along stuff, and it annoyed her to bits.

As if the music wasn't bad enough, he was singing along at the top of his voice. That finished it. She went and banged on the door of his caravan and yanked it open.

Mistake. He was naked, his body glistening with water, and he was towelling himself dry.

'Um—sorry,' she mumbled, and, dragging her eyes away, she slammed the door shut and stood there feeling foolish.

It opened seconds later, to reveal him in jeans, obviously dragged on over his wet skin and nothing else, and with the zip yanked more or less up. His chest was completely, tantalisingly bare.

He was standing in the doorway just above her, and her eyes were on a level with his lean, flat abdomen. She could see drops of water trapped in the fine curls that arrowed down under his zip, and his skin smelt of soap and sunshine.

She had a ridiculous urge to press her face into it and lick away the water. She yanked her eyes up to his face.

'That noise is disturbing me. I can't hear my television,' she said brusquely.

'Sorry—I had it on loud so I could hear it in the shower.'

'Good—that means you can turn it down now.'

He slouched against the doorframe, the towel dangling in his hand. 'You could always come in and listen properly,' he said with a grin that was too devastatingly sexy for her peace of mind.

She exhaled sharply. She wasn't sure what pregnant women were supposed to feel like, but she thought these crazy urges should have settled down with her changing hormones. Instead, she wanted him just as much as ever, if not more!

'I'd rather not,' she retorted. 'Anyway, I would have thought you would have grown out of that sort of thing,' she added repressively.

'Oh, you old fuddy-duddy,' he teased. 'Your trouble is it's so long since you had any fun you can't remember how!'

Old fuddy-duddy. Oh, God! It might be true, but it hurt none the less. Without a word she whirled and ran back to the cottage.

'Lissa? Lissa!'

She slammed him in the door, but he shouldered it open and followed her in, pursuing her across the kitchen and catching up with her by the back door.

'Lissa, sweetheart, what is it? What the hell have I said?'

The tears caught in her throat and she bit them back down. She wouldn't cry in front of him again—she wouldn't!

'Lissa?' he murmured. 'Darling, talk to me.'

It was the darling that did it. A huge, shuddering sob rose up in her throat, and with an anguished moan he turned her into his arms and cradled her against his still-damp chest. 'Oh, sweetheart, don't cry—what did I say?'

'You—called me—old,' she sobbed. 'I know I am, but you didn't have to—rub it in——'

He sighed, rocking her against him. 'Oh, Lissa— it was just a figure of speech. I didn't mean it like that—hell, most days I feel years older than you. It's like looking after one of my kid sisters trying to keep you out of trouble and make you look after yourself.' He tipped her chin up and looked into her tear-drenched eyes. 'Oh, darling. Don't cry, you'll get a headache——'

'I've got a headache!' she sniffed crossly. 'It's called Josh Lancaster!'

He chuckled, one large hand coming up and cradling the back of her head. Her hair was still up and he pulled out the pins, easing the band out and fanning it out over her shoulders. 'There, that's better,' he murmured, and then she felt the light whisper of his breath against her hair as his cheek rested against her head. 'It's like gold—pure, heavy gold. . .' Her hair sifted through his fingers, and he turned his head and pressed his lips against it, then again, then again, moving lightly over her hair until he trailed off on to her skin.

He kissed her brow, the soft warmth of his lips a delicious torment, then he tipped her face, anchored her hair with his other hand and claimed her lips.

A little cry was wrenched from her throat, and her arms came round him, her palms flattening against his back. She felt the place where he had scraped himself falling into the tree, and her hands soothed it, drawing a groan from deep inside him.

He turned her a little so that her hip fitted into the cradle of his thighs, and with a ragged sigh he rocked against her. He was aroused, obviously and considerably, and a sharp stab of desire and frustration made her cry out.

'You see how old and unattractive you are?' he murmured against her lips. 'Hell, woman, if I wanted you any more I think I'd die of it.'

His lips settled against hers again and with a little sigh she kissed him back, threading her hands through his damp hair and trapping him against her hungry mouth.

His hands came up and cupped her full, aching breasts, and a shudder ran through him. 'Oh, lord, Lissa, I need you,' he groaned against her skin. 'Stop playing games with me, for God's sake.'

Reality swamped her like a bucket of cold water. Why was she letting him do this, encouraging him, when she had no intention of marrying him or having any other close relationship with him except through the baby? It wasn't fair, and with a massive effort of will she pulled away.

'Lissa?' he murmured, reaching for her.

She took another step back, then another until she came up hard against the kitchen cupboards. 'I'm sorry,' she whispered. 'You do things to me so that I don't have any control over my own mind. I'm not playing games with you, Josh, any more than you're playing games with me. It's just what happens between us.'

He regarded her steadily. 'Then let's go to bed,' he said gruffly.

'No! I can't! Josh, please. . .!'

Her eyes locked with his, and after a long, aching moment he looked away and jammed his hands through his hair.

'Damn you, Lissa. Why me?' he whispered harshly.

She didn't know what to say. There didn't seem to be anything useful she could say, so she said nothing.

His hands dropped to his sides and he straightened up, and as he did so she saw the scrape on his back. It looked angry and sore, and she reached out tentatively and touched it.

'Leave it, Lissa,' he said roughly.

'But it's——'

'I said leave it!'

He pushed past her, yanking open the door, and as he went through it he looked back at her and his face was rigid with strain. 'I should lock your door,' he advised, and then he was gone.

She didn't lock it. God knows why, but she couldn't bring herself to shut him out.

It didn't matter, because he didn't come back anyway, and in the morning when she woke he was gone.

They walked round each other like prize fighters for the next week, wary and watchful, neither able to trust the other. On the occasions they were forced to work together they were careful not to touch, and if they did one of them usually jumped a mile.

'Why don't you just have done with it and marry him?' Anna asked in exasperation one day. 'You can't leave each other alone!'

'We never touch each other!' Melissa protested, shocked.

Anna snorted. 'Not much. And every time you do

you generate enough electricity to power the National Grid for a fortnight! Why don't you just get on with it?'

Melissa gave a short sigh. 'Because he only wants me for the baby——'

Anna folded double and laughed till the tears ran down her cheeks. 'What?' she croaked. 'Dear me, Melissa, if you believe that you'll believe anything! Either the guy has a hell of a fetish about pregnant women, or he wants you despite the fact that you're pregnant, but you mark my words, when he gets that look in his eye the baby ain't got nothin' to do with it!'

Melissa blushed furiously, but she didn't bother to argue any more. Certainly they still had a hefty dollop of sexual chemistry, but it couldn't overcome their other problems—like her age, for instance.

So she kept even more distance between them, and when they were at home she avoided him like the plague.

There was another person she was avoiding like the plague, and that was Kathleen Lawrence, the A and E sister who was blissfully happily married to Jack Lawrence, the A and E consultant, and expecting their first baby at about the same time as Melissa.

Kathleen was floating about with that nauseating, slightly bovine look of contentment that some pregnant women got, as if the world was a wonderful place and everything in it a miracle.

For Melissa, struggling with her emotions and wishing Josh were a million light-years away, Kathleen's happiness was like rubbing salt into a wound. Whenever she saw her, in the canteen for instance, she went the other way.

One day, though, she was trapped because Kath came through a door as Melissa was going the other way, and it would have been impossible to avoid her.

'Hi,' Kath said with a cheery smile. 'How's it going?'

'Oh—OK. How are you?'

'Brilliant—wonderful. I love it. Hey, listen, I was going to ask you, are you going to childbirth classes here?'

Melissa's heart sank. 'Yes—yes, I am. Are you?'

'Yes—oh, I'm really glad there's going to be someone there I know. I must dash, I have to take some bloods to the lab on my way to lunch—I'll see you!'

So much for avoiding her.

Melissa's last day at work drew nearer, and she grew more and more worried about how she would cope with the emptiness. She could only focus on the baby for so long, after all.

When the end of her last shift finally arrived, they all gathered together in her office to say goodbye. Anna handed her a parcel, prettily wrapped in baby paper, and she opened it with trembling fingers.

There were two all-in-one suits, two vests and wrapped inside them was a baby alarm, so she could listen to the baby while she was downstairs or in the garden.

'We know what a worrier you are,' Anna said, 'and we wanted to give you something useful.'

Her eyes filled. 'I don't know what to say—oh, blast. . .' She scrubbed her cheeks, gave them all a watery smile and tried again. 'I'm really going to miss you all.'

'You can come back—why don't you drop in? The kids'll miss you reading, and if you've got nothing better to do you could come and argue with Simon.' Anna's grin was a bit hit-and-miss, too, and impulsively Melissa hugged her.

'Thanks for everything,' she mumbled, and then she hugged them all in turn.

The phone rang, and one by one they all

disappeared, some to go home, others back to work, and finally she was left alone in her office.

She scooped her rubbish out of the drawers and dropped it into a carrier bag. She could sort it out at home.

She had just shut the last drawer when the door opened and closed softly.

'Are you OK?'

She looked up at Josh and managed a weak smile. 'I'm going to miss it.'

'Aren't you coming back?' he asked, perching on the edge of the desk.

'I wasn't. I don't know now. I'll have to see how I get on and if I go stir-crazy looking after the baby.' She looked up and met his eyes. 'Why? I suppose you have an opinion on it?'

He gave a short laugh. 'That rather depends on whether I'm involved, doesn't it?'

She snorted. 'That's never stopped you having an opinion in the past,' she retorted.

He gave a heavy sigh and stabbed his fingers through his hair, shrugging away from the desk. 'For what it's worth, I think you have to do what works for you as an individual. If money's a problem, it needn't be. I have every intention of supporting you and the baby——'

'That isn't necessary——'

'Let me be the judge of that, please!' he said sharply. 'It's my baby——'

'If you say that once more I think I'm going to scream!'

She slammed the drawer shut and stood up, gathering her things together, but he was standing between her and her escape route.

'Excuse me,' she muttered tightly.

With a sigh he moved out of her way, and as she

opened the door she saw a row of children lined up waiting.

Simon in his wheelchair was at the front.

'Um—we wanted to say goodbye,' he told her awkwardly. 'We've made you some stuff.'

One by one the older children gave her cards, little hanging ornaments and so on. Then Simon handed her an awkward package.

'Here,' Josh said quietly, and took the things from her so she had two hands free to open Simon's present.

It was a mobile, hand-carved in balsa wood and painted and varnished. He had made it in occupational therapy, and her eyes filled and another crop of tears ran down her cheeks.

'Oh, kids,' she said, biting her lip, and they all shuffled awkwardly.

'Heck, don't cry, Sister,' Simon mumbled, clearly embarrassed.

She sniffed and grinned. 'I'm not. I promise. It's just a cold.' She gulped a bit, and smiled again. 'Thank you, all of you, and take care, now. Be good for the new sister—don't give her any aggravation, mind.'

There were jeers and cat-calls, and she shook her head, scooped up all her presents and thanked them again, then left, accompanied by Josh carrying all the other bits and pieces.

'Just imagine Simon making me that mobile,' she said in wonder as they walked along the corridor. 'After the hard time I've given him, too.'

Josh chuckled. 'Hard time? You dote on the boy.'

She smiled fondly, pushing the outside door open with her hip. 'I suppose I do. Oh, well, you'll have to manage without me now.'

He was silent for a moment, then said softly, 'Yes. Yes, I suppose we will. Will you be all right going home on your own?'

'Of course I will,' she replied, opening her car and piling things into it. 'Josh, I don't need a keeper!'

'Don't you?' he said enigmatically, and then, handing her the last of her things, he turned and went back inside without another word.

Tuesday and her first childbirth class came all too soon. She learnt to relax, and almost fell asleep in the class.

Afterwards she refused Kath Lawrence's invitation to go for coffee at their house, and rather diffidently made her way to the children's ward.

'Yo, Sister Shaw!' Simon yelled as she went on to the ward. He skidded up to her in his wheelchair, whipped it round sideways and came to rest beside her, grinning up into her face. 'Cool, eh?'

'Ultra-cool. How are you?'

'Oh—bored, you know. There's nothing to do. Lucien's gone home, and there isn't anybody here of my age any more.'

'So you're being even more of a nuisance than usual, are you?' she said with a grin.

He rolled his eyes. 'You should see the new sister— she's really gross.' He made a retching noise and stuck his fingers in his mouth, and Melissa giggled and smacked his hand lightly.

'Simon, behave! You are so awful——'

'Can I help you?'

She straightened up, the smile dying, and saw a tall, statuesque woman in sister's uniform, her face poker-straight. 'Hello,' she said with a trace of uncertainty. 'I'm Sister Shaw—you've just taken over from me.'

The woman's eyes flicked over Melissa and returned to her face, touched with contempt. 'I see. What can I do for you?'

'Oh. . .' She shrugged. 'I just thought I'd come back and see the kids.'

'My dear, I assure you we can cope perfectly well without you,' she was told.

'Oh, I'm sure—I didn't mean to imply—— I just wondered how they all were.'

'She misses us,' Simon chipped in.

'I find that hard to believe,' the dragon said coldly.

Melissa stared at her. She herself had said such things, but never without the slightest trace of a smile.

'Actually,' she corrected, 'I do miss them. They're good kids. Simon, especially, can be a great help.'

Her eyebrows nearly fell off the back of her immaculately manicured hairstyle.

'I find that even harder to believe,' she said. 'However, fortunately I don't have to put up with them for long. Your replacement starts next week—I've been brought in just for this week as she was unwell. I imagine the thought was too much for her. You need the constitution of an ox to survive this crowd.'

And with that she turned on her heel and stalked off, leaving Simon staring at Melissa open-mouthed.

'She's not the real one! Oh, yipes, that's the best news I've had in months!'

Melissa couldn't help but laugh.

To her surprise, Melissa found she enjoyed her maternity leave. She was tired, more tired than she had realised, and she found she focused in on the baby almost to the exclusion of everything else.

Almost. One person penetrated her maternal haze without fail, just by breathing. She hardly saw him much to speak to, but at least twice a week he went shopping for her and delivered her groceries to the kitchen, refusing to take any money.

Other than that and enquiring after her health, Josh

left her alone—a fact which she found difficult to cope with. She discovered she wanted to share things with him—the information from her childbirth classes, for instance, or what Jo had said at her latest antenatal check.

And she also wanted to buy him a Christmas present.

What, though? What did you give the father of your child when you were just waiting for the baby to be born before he disappeared?

Running shoes?

In the end she bought him some gloves because she noticed he never had any and always came in rubbing his hands and complaining of the cold.

They were soft leather ones, hideously expensive but the sort of present that could have cost anything and so wouldn't embarrass him.

She also bought some handmade Belgian chocolates for his parents, and little presents for his nephew and nieces. She had decided to go to his parents' for Christmas, but she wasn't sure if the invitation was still open. Since the night he had told her to stop playing games with him they had hardly spoken, and certainly not sat down together and chatted as they had in the past.

She missed that more than anything.

Three days before Christmas she was up in the baby's bedroom trying to hang wallpaper when he came back.

She saw the car headlights through the window, then the outside light came on. Moments later he was in the bedroom beside her.

'Lissa, what the hell are you doing standing on a ladder when there's no one in the house?'

He took the length of soggy wallpaper from her, reached up the wall and placed it perfectly without the benefit of the steps, then slapped it into place with professional speed and trimmed it neatly.

'Well?'

She shrugged. 'I was hanging wallpaper.'

'I see that. Your baby's due in a week. You cannot be so silly.'

'Someone had to do it——'

'Well, not you, Lissa, and not at this point.'

'But I wanted to do it! It was important that I should do it——'

'Not more important than the baby,' he argued with irrefutable logic. She came down the ladder and poked her tongue out at his back, but he saw in the darkened window.

'Cheeky wench. Mum says, have you decided about Christmas yet?' he added as he slapped paste on to the next length.

She watched him, feeling usurped and redundant. 'Am I still welcome?'

His eyes narrowed and he looked up at her. 'Of course you are. Why shouldn't you be?'

She shrugged. 'Because you're avoiding me?'

He snorted softly. 'Forgive me. I thought we were avoiding each other.'

Their eyes locked, and then with a muttered curse he finished pasting the length and lifted it into position.

'I'll make some tea,' she offered, and escaped.

By the time she returned he had almost finished the little room and was just starting the difficult wall with the window and radiator. He paused for the tea, then she went to prepare a meal while he finished.

In fact she was pleased to stop, because her back was aching and her legs felt tired and she was generally ready to give up—apart from finding it incredibly difficult to reach the skirting board! He was also doing it better than her. That wasn't the point. She had wanted to do it for her baby—and she had a frieze to put up round the top, in pink and blue and green on a yellow background to match the mottled yellow paper. It was a lovely sunny scheme, suitable for either a boy or a girl, although of course she knew it was a girl just by instinct.

No doubt if it should turn out to be a boy Josh would make some remark about confusing his gender by not having a blue room, but she couldn't help that. She wanted her daughter—or son—to have a sunny, cheerful room, and blue was cold.

Anyway, there was blue in the frieze, though how she would get it up without going on the stepladder was a mystery to her. She'd have to do it later.

Over supper she asked him how Simon was getting on.

'Oh, OK, I suppose. He's got a friend now—another boy of thirteen who was scrumping apples and jumped off the orchard wall and shattered his heels. He'll be in for weeks too. He's had two ops to graft some bone, but he's in a pretty sorry state. Simon, on the other hand, looks as though his tibia is finally laying down some callus, so with any luck he should start to make progress now. About time—it's been ages.'

'Six months. He was in a dreadful state when he came in. I really thought he was going to lose that leg.'

'Mmm. I gather Nick Davidson did, too. He said he nearly took it off in October, but decided to give it one more try. It'll never be quite the same, but it beats an artificial leg hands down, I should say.'

They shared a smile, the first in ages, and Melissa looked quickly away.

'Anyone else?'

'Yes—more orthopaedics. Another boy, younger, who fell out of a tree this week and broke his neck. He was damn lucky. He's in a neck brace for weeks but it was an undisplaced fracture and so we're keeping him rather than transferring him and risking the journey. He's very quiet and withdrawn, though—he's a bit of a worry. Perhaps the magic show will cheer him up.'

Josh was planning a show for Christmas evening, and Melissa was looking forward to seeing all the children again—if she was still around and hadn't had the baby by then. She honestly couldn't believe she could get much bigger.

The following evening Josh turned up at her door with a Christmas tree, a set of coloured lights and lots of pretty tree decorations, and while she sat and directed operations, he put up the tree in the corner and festooned it with goodies.

'I don't really need a tree,' she had protested.

'Rubbish. What about when you come home from hospital with the baby? You have to have a Christmas tree.'

She laughed. 'Josh, you are ridiculous. It'll be a week old!'

'My child will be discerning,' he said in a tone that brooked no argument.

She didn't want to bother, anyway. The tree was lovely, and it had been years since she had really celebrated Christmas, so she settled back and said, 'Left a bit. . .how about that branch?. . .fine. No, you need some red there,' and so on while he obeyed her instructions with a long-suffering air of one hard done by.

Then he went, but he left something of himself behind and she curled up and looked at the tree and didn't feel so alone.

On Christmas morning, when she was wondering which of her rather tired maternity dresses she should wear for the day, there was a knock on the door.

She went down in her dressing-gown, stretched almost beyond capacity over her bump, and found Josh standing there with a huge, oddly shaped parcel on the ground at his feet.

'Happy Christmas,' he said with a tentative smile.

She looked from him to the parcel and back again. 'Whatever is it?'

'You'll have to unwrap it. Here, let me bring it in before we let all the heat out.'

He struggled through the narrow doorways with the mysterious parcel and set it down in front of the tree.

'Well, open it, then,' he chivvied.

She did, ripping off the huge sheets of paper to reveal a beautiful antique swinging crib.

'Oh, Josh,' she breathed. 'Oh, it's lovely! Where did you find it?'

'In a junk shop. I've been doing it up at the farm. You can stop it swinging—there's a peg you can push in. I saw one with rockers, but I didn't think it would be safe for Calico's tail.'

She ran her hand over the wood, satin-smooth and warm with the patina of age. 'Oh, it's gorgeous—oh, Josh, thank you!'

She flung herself into his arms, hugging him hard, and between them she felt the baby kick.

His eyes bright, he laid a hand over her tummy and smiled tenderly. 'Happy Christmas, baby,' he murmured.

Melancholy overwhelmed her, and with a sniff she pulled away.

'Here—I've got you something. Under the tree. It's nothing much—nothing like this.'

He grinned. 'What would I want with a crib, Lissa?'

He stooped and picked up his present, squashing it and shaking it like a kid. 'Just open it,' she told him, anticipating his disappointment.

She was way off beam. He pulled the gloves out of the paper and laughed. 'Gloves! How did you know?'

He tugged them on, smoothing the butter-soft leather against his cheek, and shook his head. 'You're a naughty girl. They're lovely—thank you.' He hugged her gently, then dropped a kiss on her forehead before releasing her.

'I ought to let you get ready—what time will you be ready to leave?' he asked.

She shrugged, suddenly awash with doubts about meeting his family. 'Whenever you think. I don't know what to wear.'

He could have just dismissed her worries, but he didn't, as if he knew how important it was for her to make a good impression.

'How about the one with flowers all over it?'

'I always wear that one.'

He grinned. 'Because you're comfortable in it, and you're comfortable in it because you look good in it. Wear it. For me. And leave your hair down.'

So she did, and despite her advanced stage of pregnancy she felt feminine and beautiful—and scared to death.

'You'll be fine,' he assured her, and she was. His family were wonderful and made her feel thoroughly at home, and to her embarrassment showered her with presents.

'Oh, but I haven't got you anything!' she said in distress, and they laughed.

'We aren't pregnant,' they told her, and then she noticed that the presents were all done up in baby paper, so she relaxed.

For the most part they were simple gifts, useful items of nursery equipment, but Hannah had painted a picture for the baby's room which she laughingly said would be worth thousands in years to come, and Mrs Lancaster had made beautiful lace cotbumpers and drapes for the crib Josh had given her.

She was overwhelmed by their generosity and welcome, and Josh ended up mopping her up again and again.

'I don't know what's the matter with me—I never cry,' she mumbled.

'Pregnancy—turns all women into watering cans,' Josh's father said sagely. 'Don't worry, it passes.'

Josh, too, received all sorts of presents because his birthday followed Christmas with indecent haste. She was relieved that no one else gave him gloves, and when they went out for a stroll and he wore them she was glad she'd given them to him.

It was a lovely day, and with one exception nobody said anything about her single status and her refusal to marry Josh.

The exception was Ellie, and when she took their four-month-old daughter upstairs to feed her and change her nappy she took Melissa too.

'I don't know why you won't marry Josh,' she said directly. 'I can see you love him, and I know he loves you. You're making him so unhappy.'

Melissa twisted her fingers together and bit her lip. 'I wish I could—you're right, I do love him, of course I do. I just daren't trust his feelings. What if he leaves me?'

Ellie stared at her in amazement. 'Leaves? Josh? Don't be ridiculous. He's the most honest, decent, faithful, loyal person I know, and that includes my husband! There's no way he'll leave you.'

'We'll see,' Melissa said quietly.

'Are you just testing him?' Ellie asked accusingly.

'No—no, I'm not. I'm giving him time to change his mind before any of us get too badly hurt.'

'He won't,' Ellie said.

'We'll see,' Melissa said again, and went back downstairs.

They left shortly after that, taking Bella with them, because Josh had to be at the hospital by six for the magic show.

Melissa was due to go with him, but she had been suffering cramping pains all afternoon, and wondered if she might have another lesion beginning to give way.

The pain seemed almost constant, just an uncomfortable niggle, and she didn't feel like sitting through the show.

'You have to come—the kids won't forgive me if I don't take you,' he told her, so she went with him and Bella, who was as good as gold.

The ward had been turned on its head for the occasion. Those children who could get out of bed were grouped round on beanbags and chairs, and those who were still bedridden were placed so they could see, unless they were too ill or too small to appreciate the entertainment.

Melissa greeted all the children she remembered— Simon in particular. 'I've got a crib for the baby—I can hang your mobile on it,' she told him. 'And I knitted you this.' She handed him a present, and he unwrapped it to reveal a jade-green sock that said 'COOL DUDE' on the top in purple capitals. 'It should fit over your plaster cast,' she told him.

'Yo, Sister!' he said with a grin, and put it on his plastered foot with glee. 'Hey, Rocky, look at this!' He stuck it out for everyone to admire, and then a hush fell because Josh appeared, clad in a black cloak with a red lining, and trailing Bella.

'Happy Christmas!' he yelled to all the children.

'Happy Christmas!' they yelled back.

He went through the 'I can't hear you' routine, and they got louder and louder until finally he was satisfied.

'Right, now, before I do anything—— Oh, what was that?'

He produced an egg from behind his ear, then another, until he had a pile of them on the table in front of him.

'How about an omelette?' he asked, and, breaking the eggs, he produced a mass of silk squares.

He did some knotting tricks with them, then he walked round the side of the table and fell over Bella.

He stared at her in astonishment. 'I forgot—ladies and gentlemen, boys and girls, I'd like to introduce you to Bella, my rabbit.'

'She's a dog,' someone yelled.

'No, she's not, she's a rabbit,' he challenged.

'Oh, no, she isn't,' an adult called from the back.

'Oh, yes, she is,' Josh countered.

'Oh, no, she isn't,' the kids all yelled.

This went on in the usual way, then Josh turned and looked at Bella, who looked soulfully back at him.

'I know—I'll ask her. One bark for yes, two barks for no, OK?'

She barked once, and the children laughed.

'Are you a rabbit? Yes?'

She barked once.

'Are you a dog?'

She barked twice.

'There you have it,' Josh announced. 'Straight from the horse's mouth!'

The kids doubled up. 'She's not a horse,' Simon yelled.

Josh put his hands on his hips, in his element. 'Did I say she was?'

'Yes,' the children shouted.

'Oh, no, I didn't!'

Off they went again. Melissa was uncomfortable, and stood up to move round a little. She was sitting at the back and didn't disturb anybody. She went into one of the side-wards, where a child in a neck brace was lying looking very sorry for himself. He was alone, and he looked lost and unhappy. He must be the boy Josh had talked about, she thought.

'Hi,' she said softly, pulling up a chair. 'Your parents gone home?'

He nodded. 'They had to give the others supper and put them to bed. It doesn't matter.'

'Didn't you want to watch the show?'

'I can't turn my head or lift it,' he told her, 'so there's no point. It sounds fun, though.'

She had an idea. 'You've got a mirror over your bed—we could tip it so you could see. Shall we try?'

She took the brakes off the bed, opened the door and pulled the bed out into the ward.

Anna caught her, pushed her out of the way and took over, and between them they got the child into a position where he could see what Josh was doing.

After a moment he giggled, and Anna stared at him in amazement.

'You're a miracle worker. He didn't want to come out here, and that's the first time he's smiled since he came in last week,' she told Melissa in an undertone.

Hearing that, she was glad she had come, even if only for the boy's sake. Her back was aching, but she didn't want to sit down. Leaving the boy with Anna, she wandered out into the corridor and walked gently up and down.

The pain was getting worse. Surely the lesion would tear soon and give her some relief?

One wall of the corridor was glass, and she rested her forehead against it and closed her eyes. It was blissfully cool and she rubbed her aching back and wondered how much longer Josh would be.

She heard clapping and cheering in the background, then footsteps striding down the corridor towards her.

Familiar footsteps—beloved footsteps. She lifted her head.

'Are you all right? I've been worried to death since you disappeared. What the hell did you think you were doing moving that bed?'

She looked at his troubled face and smiled gently. 'He was lonely. I'm OK—just backache and a lesion that won't give way. I'll be all right; it's easing a bit.'

Just then the pain returned, and with it a sensation of pressure. Her eyes widened. 'Oh,' she said.

'Stay here,' she was told, and moments later he was back.

'I've nicked Simon's wheelchair—get in. I'm taking you to Maternity.'

CHAPTER TEN

MELISSA didn't suggest he should go with her into the labour ward, and so Josh rang his parents and asked them to come to the hospital and pick up Bella, who was having a wonderful time being patted by all the children under the watchful eye of Simon, who had taken a proprietorial interest in her.

Josh took his wheelchair back and checked that everything was all right, then went back to Maternity and settled down for a long wait.

As he climbed the last flight of stairs he heard Melissa scream his name, and, thrusting aside the double doors, he ran into the ward.

There was a nurse he knew from his professional visits to the ward, standing at the desk in the middle, and Josh grabbed her by the shoulders. 'Where's Melissa Shaw?' he demanded.

'In the delivery-room, but she hasn't had the baby yet. Did they call you?'

'Not exactly,' he muttered. He spun on his heel. The delivery-room—which one? There were two.

A door opened and William Parry, one of the consultants, emerged. 'Josh, I'm glad you're here—Melissa's asking for you.'

'Is she all right?'

'Yes, she's fine. Nearly there, though.'

'Oh, God. . .' He shouldered the man out of the way and went into the room to find Melissa in a gown open all down the back, propped against the wall, moaning.

'I'm here, sweetheart—Lissa, it's OK.'

She turned into his arms, sagging against him and keening softly. His hands found the soft skin of her back and rubbed it gently, trying to soothe her. The keening turned into a sob, and then a grunt, and the doctor was back beside them.

'She needs to crouch—can you support her?'

He nodded. 'Tell me what to do.'

They locked Melissa's arms round his neck, his arms under hers and locked round her back, and let her hang, feet flat on the floor.

His muscles burned, but there was something so incredibly right about holding her while she gave birth to his son—or daughter. Lord, only a few more minutes and he would know. Not that it mattered——

Melissa cried out, and his arms tightened, holding her closer. 'It's all right, darling, I'm here,' he murmured in her ear. 'You're doing fine.'

'Pant, Melissa—that's it. Just let it come—lovely!'

The midwife caught the baby, lowered it to the mattress on the floor and helped Josh ease Melissa down.

'It's a boy—with good lungs!' Bev Linari, the midwife, said, then the baby was laid over her now soft tummy, and her hands came up tentatively to touch the fragile skin.

'Oh, Josh,' she whispered, and then her eyes welled up. He knelt beside her, hardly able to believe that the tiny child draped over Melissa was anything to do with him. What had he done to deserve such a miracle?

His eyes filled, and he blinked hard but they filled again, and, giving in, he put his arms round Melissa and hugged her.

'Well done,' he murmured unsteadily.

He had to get out of the way of the midwife then, so she could do all the necessary things, and suddenly he found himself holding his son.

'Here—you're a paediatrician. . .give him a once-over, could you?' she asked. 'Just as a formality.'

He met William Parry's eyes. 'He's my son,' he said, his voice proud and incredulous.

William smiled. 'So I gather—congratulations.'

Josh laid the baby down and examined him carefully, amazed that something so perfect could have formed without any human intervention. As they do, the baby protested at the hip test, and Josh quickly wrapped him up again and cuddled him. 'Sorry, son, I'm sorry,' he murmured, and then kissed the still damp hair. So perfect, so innocent. . .

His eyes filled again, and he carried the baby over to Melissa.

'Your son,' he said, with admirable control. 'Happy Christmas, Lissa.'

Then he left her, went down to his car and drove home to his parents. They were all gathered in the kitchen when he arrived, his father just back with Bella, and they were surprised to see him.

'Joshua?' his mother said anxiously. 'Is everything all right?'

'She's had a boy,' he said, his voice cracking, and, going into her open arms, he gave in to the tears.

Someone shoved a glass of brandy into his hand, his father handed him a handkerchief and somehow he found himself in the drawing-room telling them all about it.

'He's wonderful,' he said, the tears threatening again, and Ellie sighed crossly.

'Oh, this is so stupid,' she protested. 'Why the hell won't she marry you?'

'Ellie, stay out of it, you've done enough damage,' Michael said grimly.

Ellie's shoulders drooped. 'I just tried to do something to make him happy—how was I to know she was lying?'

'If you hadn't interfered——'

'Leave it, Mike. It's not her fault,' Josh said heavily. 'I'm going home now—I've left the mobile there. They might want to contact me.'

'Just ring them and tell them where you are,' his mother suggested, but he shook his head.

'I could do with being alone, really. I just wanted to tell you all.'

He drove back to Holly Cottage, let himself into the caravan and went straight to bed. He was exhausted, both physically and emotionally, and his mind was whirling.

Oblivion was a long time coming.

Josh was on duty on Boxing Day, and the only flowers he could find were some rather weary chrysanthemums. He bought Melissa some chocolates as well, and nipped along to the maternity unit in a quiet moment.

Jo Carter was there, complaining about her timing and expressing regret at missing the event, but when Josh arrived she made a discreet exit, leaving them alone together.

Josh handed her the flowers and chocolates, and gave her a light kiss on the cheek. 'How are you?' he asked.

'Fine—the baby's lovely. Look at him.'

He hardly dared in case he made a fool of himself again, but his sentimental excesses seemed to have retreated. He turned back the covers and peered at the little fingers and toes in fascination.

'They always seem to have such scrawny legs,' he murmured.

'He'll soon grow; he's a real trencherman—I seem to be constantly feeding him.'

Josh grinned wryly. 'I expect that's my fault—I'm always hungry.'

'He's got your eyes.'

'He has?'

They were shut, so Josh had to take her word for it. 'Have you decided what to call him?' he asked cautiously.

Her smile was tentative. 'No—I thought he was a girl. I wondered if you had any suggestions.'

'Me?'

'Well, you are his father.'

Josh swallowed. 'I'll think about it. How are you feeling?'

'Wonderful—no stitches, amazingly. I'm surprised how good I feel. I thought I was going to die.'

'Don't. Simon sends his love—he says it's really cool.' Simon had also said Josh ought to marry Melissa, but he kept that to himself. There was no point in beating that issue to death—she'd had plenty of time to say yes if she wanted to.

His bleep went, calling him back to A and E, and, dropping a kiss on her forehead, he left them.

It was a child with query diabetic ketosis, with no history of diabetes but with the smell of acid drops on his breath, acute thirst, vomiting, dehydration and drowsiness. The Christmas goodies had obviously been enough to push a slowly developing situation over the brink at a stroke, and he needed urgent treatment.

Josh admitted him to the ward, set up a drip and took enough blood for all the endless tests before running in saline fast. The glucose strip test showed his blood sugar way up in the gods, so Josh started an insulin pump in via the drip to give a steady delivery and reduce the blood glucose level to safe limits.

He was still vomiting, so they passed a nasogastric tube with the child's reluctant and unhappy co-operation, and aspirated his stomach contents. The nausea eased a little, and the poor child lay exhausted while Josh discussed the case with his parents.

'He'll need an X-ray of his chest to see if he's got an infection, and we'll do cultures of his blood and urine to see if there's a source of infection there, because children sometimes have these diabetic-type reactions when they're ill.'

'So it may not be diabetes?'

Josh shook his head. 'No, it may not. It could well be, though, so we need to test him very thoroughly to find out exactly what's causing it before we make a decision. In the meantime he's out of danger, but he'll need to be in here undergoing fairly intensive treatment for some days, or maybe even weeks. I don't know if you want to stay with him, but, bearing in mind it's a strange place, we do encourage parents to be with their children as much as possible, and there's a room available for you to sleep here to be near him.'

'Please,' the woman said, and some of the worry cleared from her face. 'I know he's in good hands, but if they're out of sight you worry about them, and he looks so tiny there——'

She broke off and her husband put his arm round her and gave her a hug. 'Come on, love, he'll be all right,' he said comfortingly, and for the first time Josh really understood what it was to be a parent.

It was the most wonderful gift in the world, and at the same time the most terrifying responsibility.

How could he allow Melissa to shoulder it alone?

She came home with the baby—still unnamed—after six days. Kathleen Lawrence had had a little girl the day after Boxing Day, on their second wedding anni-

versary, and they had been together. It had been
fun in the hospital, although Jack was in there at
every available opportunity and Melissa had hardly
seen Josh.

He popped in if he was up in the unit for professional
reasons, but for the most part he didn't stay long.
Everyone wanted time off and so rotas were juggled.
Josh was saving his time off for when Melissa came
out, and, although she was glad of that later, at the
time she felt neglected.

Which was absurd, because she only had herself to
blame. She could have been married to him, instead
of feeling so lonely and unwanted.

The baby wanted her, though. He was adorable, the
best thing that had ever happened to her, and she
couldn't spend enough time with him.

Usually he cried very little, and the feeding was
going well—until someone brought her grapes when
he was eight days old.

Then he got colic, and screamed and screamed and
screamed.

She was pacing the floor with him, at her wits' end,
when Josh walked through the door and took him out
of her arms.

'Get a coat on, and some boots, and go out
for a walk,' he ordered gently. 'Go on, you need
a break.'

'I'm fine,' she protested, but he shooed her out.

'I'm a paediatrician—I can handle a crying baby
with colic. Now go.'

She went, suddenly aware of how bottled-up
she'd been feeling, and had a brisk, refreshing walk
in the January sunshine. She felt much better when
she came back, and to her surprise the house was
quiet.

She tiptoed in to find Josh still walking up and down,

his shirt off and the baby, naked except for a nappy, held against his heart. Josh's big hand lay over the baby's back, keeping him warm, and his arms and legs hung like a rag doll's. He was flat out, completely exhausted, and Josh just kept gently walking, letting him rest.

Melissa curled up in her chair and watched as Josh cradled his son against his heart and murmured soothingly to him whenever he twitched.

Finally Josh laid him down in the crib and rocked it gently. The baby hardly stirred.

'I think he's OK now. He had a horrendous nappy.'

'I'm sorry. I should have been here——'

Josh gave her a wry, sad smile. 'He's my son, too, Melissa. Why should you have all the fun?'

She looked away. His eyes were so expressive. She felt tears clogging her throat. Why didn't she just marry him and have done with it?

Because he'd leave her. She knew it.

'Have you thought about his name?' she asked to change the subject.

He hesitated. 'I thought—maybe Benedict. It means blessed. He was born on Christmas Day—that must be significant.'

His voice was choked, and Melissa just nodded. She couldn't speak.

Josh slowly stopped rocking the crib and stood up. 'He's all right now.'

'Thank you for settling him and giving me a break. I needed it.' She stood up as well, and handed him the bag of grapes. 'Here, take these with you. I mustn't eat any more. I didn't realise they'd upset him.'

He took the bag. 'You know where I am if you need me,' he said gruffly, and then he let himself out.

She went over to the crib and looked down at their son. Benedict.

She tried it aloud. 'Benedict. Ben.'

It suited him.

Josh looked up from digging the garden and saw Melissa sitting in the corner of the settee, feeding Ben. She looked beautiful, her hair tucked behind her shoulder like golden rain, her soft, full breast blue-veined and ripe with motherhood, Ben's little fist curled against it.

It brought an ache to his heart. It was a familiar ache, one he'd felt a lot recently in the four weeks since his son's birth.

'What the hell are you doing here, Lancaster?' he asked himself. 'Lying outside her house like a slave draped over the doorstep, guarding her from ills real and imagined.' He gave a choked laugh. He must be crazy. 'She doesn't need you,' he muttered. 'She's got what she wanted—why the hell don't you just leave her to it?'

He finished edging the border, put the spade back in the shed and went back round to the front.

He rang his father. 'Can I borrow the Range Rover?' he asked.

'Of course. When do you want it? I have to come to town now—do you want me to drop it over to you?'

'Could you? Thanks.'

He didn't ask any more. Josh was glad. He didn't feel he could talk about it.

He went into the caravan, packed up all the loose gear and put everything away. The water needed emptying, and the gas bottle had to be turned off. His father turned up and switched cars without a word. One look at his son's face had been enough. He simply patted him on the shoulder and went.

Josh backed up the Range Rover, connected up the tow hitch and lights, and wound up the stabilising legs on the back of the caravan. There was one last thing to do, and he took a steadying breath. Melissa was standing in the window watching him, her arms wrapped round her waist, and her face was a mask. He walked to the door.

There was a tap on the door, and after a moment she opened it, her heart leaden in her chest.

'I need to unplug the extension lead,' he told her.

'You're going, aren't you,' she said. It wasn't a question.

'You don't need me any more, Lissa,' he said quietly. 'You and Ben are fine without me. It's time for all of us to get on with our lives.'

He passed the lead out of the window and shut it again, then turned back to her.

'I'll be around to see how you're getting on, and to see Ben.' He hesitated, as if there was something else he wanted to say, but then without a word he went out and closed the door.

She watched him from the window as he passed the lead into the caravan and secured it, then got into the car.

He put his seatbelt on, started the engine and then he turned to wave. Suddenly she couldn't bear it.

'No!' she cried. 'Josh, no!'

She ran to the door and yanked it open just as the engine started and the caravan started to move. 'Josh, wait!' she screamed.

She ran after him, banging on the side of the caravan. 'Josh!'

He stopped and got out, his face wary.

'Lissa?'

'Stay,' she begged. 'Please, Josh, stay. . .'

He closed his eyes. 'Lissa, I can't——'

Pain swamped her. 'I knew you'd go,' she wept.

'I just didn't know it could hurt like this.'

His hands were on her shoulders, warm and comforting. 'Lissa, you'll be all right, you can cope. You don't need me now——'

'I do! I've always needed you. I was just afraid to love you in case you left me. . .' She fell against his chest, gripping his clothes with her hands and clinging to him. 'Don't go, Josh—please, don't go! I love you.'

'Oh, Lissa——' His arms were round her like steel bands, wrapping her against his chest, his mouth finding hers and clinging as if he would die without her.

A sob rose in her throat, and, breaking the kiss, he scooped her into his arms and carried her inside, kicking the door shut behind him. 'Where's Ben?'

'In the crib,' she told him, scrubbing the tears off her face. 'Why?'

'Is he asleep?'

'Yes.'

'Good—because I'm taking you to bed right now.'

Panic filled her. The birth had been easy, but it wasn't very long ago and she wasn't sure she was ready yet.

'Josh, I don't think——' she began, but he interrupted her.

'Good. You do too much thinking. Just feel for once.'

He put her down on the edge of the bed, stripped his clothes off down to his briefs and then eased her dress over her head.

'Josh, I can't——'

'I know that,' he said softly. 'I just need to hold you. Please, Lissa.'

He took her hands and pulled her gently to her feet, then turned back the quilt and pushed her back into the bed, sliding in beside her. Then his arms closed round her and he sighed.

'Do you have any idea how much I've longed to hold you?' he murmured. 'I've watched you with Ben, seen the way your relationship with him is growing, and all the time I've been on the outside. I thought if you wanted me you'd ask——'

He broke off, his throat working, and Melissa stared at him in puzzlement.

'I didn't think you wanted us,' she said slowly. 'In the hospital, when he was born, you gave him to me, said, "Your son," and left, just like that. I didn't know where you'd gone—I thought you didn't care.'

'I couldn't take it. I wanted you both so badly I just wanted to break down and cry, and I didn't want to put that kind of pressure on you.'

'And I thought you didn't really care,' she sighed.

'Of course I cared—I'll always care. There didn't seem to be anything I could say to you. I didn't know how to convince you I was sincere,' he said heavily. 'I knew you didn't trust me, and I thought if I gave you time you'd realise I meant what I said and ask me to stay, but you didn't. Then today I watched you feeding Ben and I just wanted to run away. I couldn't take it any more, Lissa. . .'

Tears clumped on his lashes, and she reached up and kissed them away. 'Oh, Josh, I'm so sorry. I thought you'd get bored, or go off me. My figure's shot to bits now, I'm much older than you, I probably can't have another child—I couldn't see what you'd want with me.'

'Silly girl—I love you,' he murmured unsteadily. 'I don't care about your figure, or having any more babies, and your age is neither here nor there. You're only three years older than me.'

'Four.'

'Three. I'm thirty-one now, you're thirty-four. That's three,' he argued.

'Till July.'

'That's miles away,' he said with a tender smile, and kissed her. 'Anyway, none of it matters because I love you. That's the only thing that matters any more. That and Ben.'

'I haven't registered his birth yet,' she said softly. 'I wanted to ask you to come with me so we can register him in your name.'

His arms tightened fractionally. 'Maybe we could get married and have him christened and do it all on the same day to save time,' he suggested warily.

She tipped her head back and met his eyes. 'Really?' she whispered.

'That's what I'd like—given a choice.'

A slow, radiant smile lit her face. 'That's what I'd like, too, given a choice, but we'll have to be quick. His birth has to be registered within six weeks, and we've only got two left.'

'No problem. I didn't intend to give you too long— you might change your mind.' Josh reached out a hand and picked up her bedside phone, punching in some numbers.

'Mum? It's Josh. When Dad gets back with my car, can you turn him round and send him back to collect the caravan? I don't need it any more.'

She heard a voice on the other end, and his eyes locked with Melissa's. 'I'm going to be where I belong—with my wife and child,' he said into the phone. Then he laughed and said, 'Not yet. Of course you're invited. And that reminds me, how quickly can you make a wedding cake?'

He laughed again, said goodbye and hung up, then pulled Melissa back into his arms.

'That's a stroke of luck,' he told her. 'She made it when she did the Christmas cake, crafty old thing. She says she knew we'd end up together.'

'Did she? I didn't. It's a good job we didn't disappoint her,' Melissa said softly.

'No chance. She knows me. I don't give up when things are important to me. She knew I'd still be here for you.'

'But you were going!' she exclaimed.

'Only back to the hospital. There's no way you were getting rid of me for keeps, Lissa. No way!'

'Because of Ben.'

He lifted himself up on one elbow and looked down at her, his eyes the colour of midnight. 'Because of you,' he murmured, and the love in those eyes convinced her as no words ever could. 'I'm sorry, sweetheart, but I'm afraid you're stuck with both of us.'

She snuggled closer. 'I think I can just about tolerate that.'

Just then she heard Ben starting to cry, and dug Josh in the ribs. 'Hey. You hear that?'

'Mmm.'

'He needs feeding.'

'Mmm.'

'Well, get him, then.'

'Why me?' Josh mumbled. 'I'm asleep.'

She flicked the quilt off him and pushed him with her foot. 'Go on. He's your son, too.'

He grinned, rolled over and kissed her. 'So he is,' he said softly, and then, padding barefoot down the stairs, she heard him say, 'All right, little man. Daddy's here.'

She sighed with contentment. So he was—and it felt absolutely right. . .

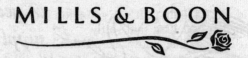

MILLS & BOON

LOVE CALL

The books for enjoyment this month are:

THAT'S MY BABY!	Caroline Anderson
A CHRISTMAS BLESSING	Marion Lennox
A VOICE IN THE DARK	Josie Metcalfe
THE GENEROUS HEART	Margaret O'Neill

———————— ❧ ————————

Treats in store!

Watch next month for the following absorbing stories:

PRESCRIPTION FOR CHANGE	Sheila Danton
REMEDY FOR PRIDE	Margaret Holt
TOTAL RECALL	Laura MacDonald
PRACTICE IN THE CLOUDS	Meredith Webber

Available from W.H. Smith, John Menzies, Volume One, Forbuoys, Martins, Tesco, Asda, Safeway and other paperback stockists.

Readers in South Africa - write to:
IBS, Private Bag X3010, Randburg 2125.

A year's supply of Mills & Boon Romances—absolutely FREE!

Would you like to win a year's supply of heartwarming and passionate romances? Well, you can and they're FREE! Simply complete the wordsearch puzzle below and send it to us by 30th June 1996. The first 5 correct entries picked after the closing date will win a years supply of Mills & Boon Romances (six books every month—worth over £100). What could be easier?

READER SERVICE
ROMANCE
RESIST
HEART
MEMORIES
PAGES
KISS
SPINE
TEMPTATION
LOVE
COLLECTION
ROSES
PACK
PARCEL
TITLES
DREAMS
COUPLE
SPECIAL EDITION
EMOTION
DESIRE
SILHOUETTE
MOODS
PASSION

M	E	R	O	W	A	L	R	L	M	S	P	C	O	S
	O		E	C	I	V	R	E	S	R	E	D	A	E	R
R	O						E		O	S	M	A	E	R	D	S
O	D	H	E	A	R	T		S		S		S	E	L	T	I	T
M	S			S		E		M	E	M	O	R	I	E	S	S
A	E			C	G			S	A		C				E
N	P	T		A		E	K		W		O	I			W
C	E		T	P	K	I	S	S	C			L	T	T		O
E			E		H		A	E	V	O	L		E	N	N
	A	E		U		M		P	R		T	E	I	M	O	E
	E	N		L	O			L	I		S	C		P	I	O
S	L	I			H	A		S		I	T		T	S	A
	P	P	A	R	C	E	L	N	E		S	I		A	S	Z
	U	S	D	B			I	D		E	O		T	A	I
O	O		O		N		B	S		R	N		I	P	S
	C		E	N	N	A	M	T	R	R	L	G	N	O	L	T
	O		E	M	O	T	I	O	N			O	N		I
N	O	I	T	I	D	E	L	A	I	C	E	P	S	K

Please turn over for details of how to enter…

How to enter

Hidden in the grid are words which relate to our books and romance. You'll find the list overleaf and they can be read backwards, forwards, up, down or diagonally. As you find each word, circle it or put a line through it.

When you have found all the words, don't forget to fill in your name and address in the space provided below and pop this page into an envelope (you don't need a stamp) and post it today. Hurry—competition ends 30th June 1996.

Mills & Boon Wordsearch
FREEPOST
Croydon
Surrey
CR9 3WZ

Are you a Reader Service Subscriber?   Yes ❏   No ❏

Ms/Mrs/Miss/Mr _____

Address _____

_____

_____ Postcode _____

One application per household.

You may be mailed with other offers from other reputable companies as a result of this application. If you would prefer not to receive such offers, please tick box. ❏

COMP295
F